CATCHING the COWGIRL

A COTTON CREEK ROMANTIC COMEDY

A COTTON CREEK ROMANTIC COMEDY

JENNIE MARTS

Entangled Publishing, LLC
2614 South Timberline Road
Suite 109
Fort Collins, CO 80525
Visit our website at www.entangledpublishing.com.

Lovestruck is an imprint of Entangled Publishing, LLC.

Edited by Brenda Chin
Cover design by Liz Pelletier
Cover art from iStock

Manufactured in the United States of America

First Edition July 2017

This book is dedicated to Todd—
The perfect catch for me
I'm so thankful we caught each other

Chapter One

One bar? One freaking bar? How far into the boonies was this place that they didn't even have decent cell phone reception?

Adam Clark held up his cell phone and watched the last bar blink away. Great.

His flight had been delayed, and he hadn't heard from either of his coworkers. Brandon and Ryan were flying in from London, and he assumed they'd be waiting for him at the ranch. At least they'd better be.

He sighed. This whole idea of spending a week at a real working dude ranch in Colorado had been Brandon's idea. He'd convinced them it would be great research for the new video game they were working on—and really, what could go wrong? Three computer guys from California acting like cowboys? It sounded like a super plan.

It wouldn't be the first dumb idea Brandon had talked him into. The three of them had met in college, rooming together in the Engineering dorm. After graduation, they'd gone into business together and had created one of the most popular video games on the market.

Their newest game would have a western theme, and Brandon had decided they needed to "experience the real West" if the game was going to feel authentic.

All Adam could feel right now was hot and uncomfortable. The stiff western-style shirt stuck to his sweaty skin, and he couldn't feel his toes at all. They were squished into a pair of "genuine snakeskin" cowboy boots that the salesman had said all the cowboys in Colorado wore.

He lurched against the back of the seat in front of him as the bus turned off the winding mountain road and passed under a sign that read HAWKINS RIDGE RANCH. It looked like they'd arrived.

The bus pitched to a stop, and laughter rang out as the excited families around him stood and collected their belongings. From what he could gather, he and his friends would be spending the week with three other groups: a family celebrating their teenage daughter's birthday, another family from Florida, who wanted to try a non–amusement park vacation, and one couple celebrating their honeymoon.

He followed the honeymooners, grabbing his luggage, then stepped out of the bus and shaded his eyes from the bright Colorado sun.

The scent of pine and freshly mown grass filled the air, punctuated with a haze of dust. His throat was already dry, and he looked around, hoping to spot a place he could get a drink.

A large timber lodge sat to his right, surrounded by a scattering of small cabins. In front of him stood a huge barn, with corrals spread out on either side. Behind the barn, green fields dotted with horses and cattle completed the landscape.

A curvy blonde woman strode purposefully toward the group, a straw cowboy hat on her head and a clipboard in her hands. An older cowboy sauntered next to her, and a brooding preteen shuffled along behind them.

"Hey there," the cowgirl called, a big smile on her face. "Welcome to Hawk's Ridge Ranch. I'm Skye Hawkins. My dad built this ranch for my mother the year before I was born. Now, I'm not saying exactly what year that was—I'll just admit that this handsome twelve-year-old is my son."

Her eyes cut to Adam, and she offered him a grin.

Light laughter rippled through the crowd, but Adam just stood there, staring at the woman. Just her smile had set something off inside of him. Something about her struck a chord with him, unsettled him somehow.

He shook his head. He was here to work, nothing else.

Skye dropped an arm casually around the shoulders of the sullen preteen standing next to her. "This is Cody. He'll be showing the Henderson and the Johnson families to their cabins."

Cody gave a half-hearted wave, but it didn't escape Adam's attention that the boy's gaze darted to the cute girl who was about his age. Memories of those awkward teenage years flooded his mind. Adam felt for the kid.

"This is Cal. He's the lead ranch hand and your go-to guy for just about everything," Skye continued, gesturing to the older man standing next to her. "Cal and Cody are gonna show y'all to the mess hall, where you'll experience some of the best western barbecue you've ever tasted." She smiled at the couple wearing matching cowboy hats, with ribbons proclaiming "bride" and "groom" wrapped around their brims. "We'd like to extend a special welcome to our newlyweds, the Logan's. We're thrilled you've decided to spend your honeymoon with us. Cal will lead you to your cabin, where we've added a few special touches to make this time memorable for you."

Okay, enough with the pleasantries. Adam just wanted to get to his cabin and get started. He wondered who'd be taking him to his cabin, and he silently hoped it would the cowgirl herself.

"We know you're anxious to get settled in, so we'll save the rest of the introductions until dinner. Please check out the information packets you each have in your rooms. You'll find camp agendas, meal times, and hopefully everything you'll need to have a great week here at Hawk's Ridge Ranch." Skye glanced his way. "You must be Adam."

He nodded. "Yep."

"Good to meet you. If you want to follow me, I'll take you to your cabin." She reached for his bag.

"I've got it," he said, as he noted the absence of a wedding ring. Hmm. Being away from civilization for a week might not be so bad…

He grabbed his bag and fell into step behind her. She wore a light pink T-shirt tucked into a pair of snug-fitting jeans, their hems frayed at the bottom around the heels of her boots. A heavy brown belt with brass studs circled her waist, and though he did his best, he couldn't keep his eyes off the way her heart-shaped butt shifted with each step.

His own feet were still killing him, and he tried to focus on what she was saying instead of how badly his toes were being pinched in the stupid snakeskin cowboy boots.

Brandon had insisted they show up decked in full gear. It would help them get in the cowboy mindset, he'd said. But now, as he limped along behind Skye, Adam wished he'd just worn his usual Converse sneakers.

"I hate to break it to you, but I received a call from Brandon Moore this afternoon. He and Ryan, the other gentleman in your party, won't be joining you today."

Adam's head snapped up, the pain in his toes forgotten. "Wait. What? Brandon and Ryan aren't coming? I thought they were already here."

"From what I gathered, they couldn't make their flight from London. They said they've been trying to reach you on your cell phone. I told them reception up here is awful."

He pulled out his phone and squinted at the display. "More like non-existent. Did they say when they'd get here?"

She shook her head. "No, they weren't sure. They said to tell you there'd been some complications on the London project, something to do with a server that couldn't handle all the traffic and a massive crash, and that you'd know what that meant."

Yeah, he knew.

Brandon and Ryan had gone to London to release their newest video game, and it must have been more popular than they'd planned. They'd had five thousand preorders, but if the release had been too big, it could have crashed the server. They'd been worried that could be a problem.

But now *their* problem was going to be *his* problem. Because he was the one stuck doing a solo week at Camp Cowboy.

How had he let Brandon and Ryan talk him into this? Sure, it had made sense at the time. None of them had a clue about being a cowboy, other than what they saw on television. This week, they were supposed to learn how to ride a horse and swing a rope. They'd get a feel for what a real working ranch felt like, smelled like.

This wasn't a totally new idea for them. They'd gone on location before to research their other games, but those locations had involved beaches, beer, and women in bikinis.

Still, there was a reason Brandon was in charge of marketing and production—he could talk them into doing most anything. Adam had almost started to look forward to this trip…

But not now.

"I'm sorry about your friends. I hope no one got hurt," she said.

"Hurt?"

"In the massive crash."

"They'll be fine," he assured her. Or at least they would be, until he killed them when, and if, they ever showed up.

"That's good. Hopefully, they'll still be able to join you later this week.

They'd better. The heel of his boot caught on a rock, and he stumbled then caught his footing.

"You okay?"

"I'm fine," he grumbled. "Just not used to walking in these stupid boots."

"Yeah, they do take some getting used to. Those are some fancy boots." She didn't quite hide her amused smile.

Stupid salesman. "They were Brandon's idea. He thought we should dress the part this week. You know, western shirts, boots, the whole nine yards. But I think I blew it."

Her gaze traveled up and down his outfit. "I'd say you almost pulled it off, but the Stormtroopers on your belt give away the fact that you might not be a real cowboy."

He grimaced. "I was hoping no one would notice. I couldn't find my brown leather belt this morning, and this was the only other thing I had."

"It's kind of cool. It gives you like a 'space cowboy' kind of vibe." She let out a laugh. "So, is this your first trip to Colorado? It has a lot to offer, like the mountains, and skiing, and we've even got a pretty great football team. Go Broncos." She gave a little fist pump.

"I like the Broncos. They had a good team last year. Does your husband watch a lot of football?" Wow. That was smooth.

She cocked an eyebrow at him. "I'm not married."

"Me neither." *Shit.* "Sorry. That was clearly not the appropriate response. I meant to just say that I'm sorry."

"Don't be. Cody's dad was an asshole. I dodged a six-foot tall bullet when he walked away from us."

"Still, I know that being a single mom isn't easy. I was

raised by one. My dad was killed in a car crash when I was about your son's age."

"Oh, now I'm sorry."

He shrugged. "It was a long time ago."

"Still, I think it's different when your man intentionally walks away."

He shrugged. "I don't think either sounds preferable."

"I don't mean to sound bitter. I'm over him. I just sometimes think about how one stupid decision can alter your entire life, you know?"

He did know. "So, where would you be if you hadn't made that one decision? Still running this dude ranch?"

"God, no. I mean, don't get me wrong, I love this ranch, it's my home. And I wouldn't give up Cody for the world. But I never imagined myself back here. I had big plans. I met Cody's dad when I was in college, where I was studying equine science. I'd hoped to get into vet school and move to Montana. Then I met a cowboy who swept me off my feet, literally. I thought we were in love, that we'd get married and move to Montana together. Then I told him that I was pregnant."

"I take it that didn't go so well?"

She chuckled. "Uh, no, not so well at all. He was a rodeo guy who was in town for a circuit. Turned out he liked riding bulls better than riding me." She clapped her hands to her mouth, and a tinge of pink colored her cheeks.

He let out a loud laugh. He liked this woman. She surprised him. And he wasn't surprised by much anymore.

"Sorry, I should *not* have said that."

"It's okay. It was funny."

She grinned at him, and he felt another tug of attraction. He wasn't used to being this affected by a woman. Sure, she was pretty. Gorgeous, actually. But more important, he liked that she made him laugh, that she had spunk.

"I can't believe I'm telling my whole life story to a complete stranger."

"We're not exactly strangers. We've known each other for a good ten minutes already."

"Good point. We're practically BFFs."

BFFs? The thoughts he'd had about the way Skye's butt looked in those snug jeans didn't fall anywhere near the friends category. "Right. And BFFs don't have to be embarrassed about spilling their guts to each other. Usually they get drunk and sloppy before they start leaking their innermost secrets. So I may have to buy you a beer at the bar before you tell me anything else." He tried not to cringe. Somehow that had sounded much better in his head.

She turned the corner, leading him toward a log cabin set back against the hill side. "I'm afraid the only bars you'll find around here are the chocolate bars we sell in the gift shop."

Hmm. He wasn't sure if he'd just been dissed or if she was still trying to be funny.

"Then next time, we'll just have to get sloppy over chocolate."

"I don't think there's anything left to tell. I've already spilled my most humiliating secrets." She stopped at the bottom step of the porch to the cabin and glanced at him. "I don't usually tell anyone about Cody's dad. It's not just that I was dumped, but it changed everything in my life. I had to drop out of college and come back home with my tail between my legs. I mean, I'm fine with my life now. I love my son and wouldn't change what happened. But still, it was hard."

"You seem to be doing pretty well, in spite of it."

"Thank you. You're sweet."

He shrugged. "Not really. Apparently I'm kind of an asshole myself, sometimes. At least, according to the last woman I dated."

She continued up the stairs of the porch. "But you're not

seeing anyone now?"

She'd asked the question innocently enough, but he couldn't help the grin that stole across his face. "Nope."

"Well, here we are," she said, effectively changing the subject as she unlocked the door to the cabin. "This is Hillside. It's one of our largest cabins, so you and your friends should be comfortable."

Adam dropped his bag and set his backpack on top of it as he gazed around the sparsely furnished room. A sofa and coffee table sat in front of the cabin's main focal point, a large stone fireplace. The floor was faded hardwood covered with colorful rag rugs.

The windows were covered with blue and white gingham curtains, and a set of bunk beds sat against one wall. Two doors led off to the right. One was closed, but Adam could see a chipped porcelain sink through the other and assumed it was the bathroom.

The cabin was straight off the set of *Bonanza*. He half expected Hoss or Little Joe to come sauntering into the room.

His shoulders sagged at the thought of spending the next week here. There was no television, no refrigerator, and the sofa looked about as comfortable as a rock. At least he wouldn't be stuck sleeping on one of the bunk beds. Brandon and Ryan could share those—if they ever showed up. It would serve them right for ditching him.

"Nice place," he told Skye, who seemed to be waiting for his reaction.

When he was working, he usually stayed in four-star hotels with 24-hour business centers. But she looked so proud of the cabin he didn't want to say anything to upset her. He wasn't that much of a jerk.

"This is one of my favorite cabins." Skye fluffed a blue pillow on the sofa. "It's one of the older ones, but it's also the biggest and it's quiet, since it's set a little farther back. I think it'll work out really well for you. And for your friends, when they show up."

"Thanks. It is quiet." A slight breeze ruffled the curtains of the windows, but all he heard was the gurgling of the stream that ran behind the cabin. "That will help, because I do have a lot of work to get done while I'm here. Do I need a specific wifi password, or is it just open?"

She let out a laugh, and his stomach dropped. He had a feeling he knew what was coming.

"You don't need a password at all, because there is no wifi. The only internet access is in the main lodge, and even that is limited."

He gave her an incredulous stare. "Are you kidding me? No wifi? And no cell phone service? What kind of place is this?" The third ring of hell? How was he supposed to get any work done?

"It's the kind of place where you're supposed to forget about the real world and just enjoy being in the mountains, soaking up everything nature has to offer," she replied, planting a hand on her hip.

He arched an eyebrow at her. Unfortunately, he didn't really *do* nature. He kept in shape by working out religiously at the gym, but other than that, he spent the majority of his time at his desk, either at home or at the office.

She gave him a knowing smile. "But it's also the kind of place that leaves freshly baked chocolate chip cookies in your room to enjoy when you arrive." She pointed to the two doors. "Bedroom's through there, and bathroom's on the right."

A loud *thud* sounded in the bedroom she'd just indicated.

Those assholes. They'd made it after all.

"Nice try, you jerks," he said, walking over and flinging open the door. "You really had me going."

But the room appeared to be empty.

Adam's gaze flicked around, noting everything at once.

The room had the same log cabin decor as the rest of the cabin. A queen-size bed covered in a light-green and blue quilt sat against one wall, a matching oak night stand next to it, holding a pine cone–accented lamp and an old-fashioned alarm clock.

A small framed picture lay broken on the floor, as if it had been knocked off the wall.

Two large windows covered the top half of one wall, both open and offering a view of the mountains.

He blinked, trying to figure out what had caused the picture to break. Then he heard a fluttery sound coming from across the room, almost like the wings of a bird. He looked at the windows again. A strange gray lump seemed to hang in the middle of the curtain.

He squinted and moved toward the odd dark shape, then threw up his arms in defense as the gray lump shifted, then took off and flew right at him.

Chapter Two

What the hell?

Skye jerked back as Adam let out a curse and slammed the door to the bedroom. "What's wrong?"

"Holy frickin' crap." He took two steps back and rubbed his hands through his hair. "I thought my friends were in there. But they're not." He spoke quickly, almost spitting the words out. "There's a flipping bat in there."

"A bat? Oh shit." She crossed the room and slowly opened the door to peer inside.

A good-sized bat hung from the holes in the lace curtains. She pulled the door shut. "Yep. That's a bat all right." *Great.* Because Hillside was the largest cabin, she could charge more for it. The last thing she needed was for him to ask for his money back. Damn critter.

"It's okay. I've got this handled." She hoped she sounded more confident than she felt. "We're used to wildlife around here."

"So how do we get that thing out of my room?"

"It shouldn't be too hard." She crossed the room and

propped the front door open with a chair from the dining room table. "We'll open the place up, then wait a few minutes and see if he just flies out on his own. Easy."

He cocked an eyebrow at her. "Easy? What if it bites us? What if it has rabies or something?"

"All right, settle down there, city boy. Bats aren't mean, and they don't bite." She chuckled as she opened the front door, then crossed back to the bedroom. She sent up a silent prayer that this would work as easily as she'd tried to convince him that it would. "Stand back."

Adam held up his hands. "Wait." He moved to stand behind her and the safety of the door. "Just in case."

She grinned, then opened the bedroom door.

They waited.

Nothing happened.

Nothing except her pulse raced a little, standing this close to Adam.

What's that about?

She'd been a single mom for so long, focusing all of her energy on raising her son, that she didn't usually take notice of men. Especially ones that were guests…from California… who were only going to be there for one week.

So why was the smell of Adam's aftershave sending sparks of heat down her back? And why did she find so much about him appealing? Like how cute his smile was, how tall he was, and how muscled his forearms were. How he'd made her laugh.

And especially, how her body was heating up just from being close to him.

She looked up, surprised at how close she was actually standing to him, and even more surprised by the intense way he was looking back down at her.

At her lips.

She swallowed, her mouth suddenly dry, but not able to

tear her gaze away.

His jaw was square and defined, and a light dusting of black whiskers covered his cheeks. A tiny white scar ran vertically next to his eyebrow, and she had the sudden urge to reach up and run her finger across it.

A shock of black hair fell across his forehead. His eyes were deep brown, like dark chocolate, and seemed to peer directly into her soul.

Great, now she was turned on *and* hungry.

He swallowed, then asked, his voice almost a whisper, "What happens now? Should we wait?"

"Wait for what?" Her own voice was soft, breathy.

"For the bat?"

"The bat?" Reality crashed back into her.

Holy crap. What the hell am I doing?

She took a step back, shaking her head. "Yes. Of course, the bat. Where is it? Did it fly out?"

What the heck was wrong with her? She never acted like this.

They *had* seemed to hit it off, though, and she was sure he'd been flirting with her earlier. But just because he was cute and he'd made her laugh, that didn't mean anything was going to happen between them. They were hiding out from a bat.

For a moment there, she'd thought he was going to kiss her. He *had been* staring at her lips, looking at her mouth as if he'd wanted to consume her.

Pull it together, girl.

She peered cautiously around the edge of the door. "Shit."

"What? What's wrong? What's it doing?" Adam leaned over her shoulder, his chest practically touching her back as he tried to see around the door. "It's just hanging there."

The bat hadn't moved.

"I think we're going to need to persuade it to leave," she

said.

"Like how?"

"Go on. Git," she hollered at the animal, waving her arms as if to guide him to the open front door.

The bat continued to hang there, unfazed.

She tried again, this time leaning forward in an aggressive stance and raising her voice even louder. "Git on outta here, now!"

Her more assertive stance must have freaked the bat out, because it took off. She leaped back, trying to get out of its way.

"I told you. Bats are crazy," he yelled, pressing himself against the wall as the bat flew around the room.

"Okay, calm down." She tried for a teasing tone. "Don't tell me you're afraid of a little bat?"

"Not afraid, no. But icked out, yes." He shivered. "They're cool to study, but I don't enjoy being in the room when one's flying around. You know those little suckers can fly up to sixty miles an hour? They are so adept that they can make a right-hand turn the length of their own body at forty miles an hour."

"Yes, but they also use echo location, so they can fly through a forest in complete darkness. So you don't have to worry. If they can miss a tree, they're not going to fly into you."

"I'm not taking that chance."

She chuckled. "You know there's a popular superhero who has a thing for bats. Imagine you're him."

"That won't work. The great parts about him are his suit and his car and his cool gravelly voice. Just because I like him, that doesn't mean I like the creepy little beasts."

She grinned. "Bats are important because they're pollinators and they eat insects, especially mosquitoes. They can actually eat like twelve hundred mosquitoes in an hour. And they can consume their body weight in insects every night."

"Okay, now you're just showing off." He let out a soft chuckle, and his shoulders relaxed a little.

She laughed with him, thankful that his attention was focused on her and not the bat. "That, and I have a friend who's a park ranger. He comes up every few weeks and does a great program on bats for our guests. I've heard it several times now, so I've picked up on a few things."

"Okay, then, Ms. Holder of Bat Wisdom. What do we do now?" he asked, his back still against the wall.

"I don't think he'll leave on his own if we're still in the room. We need to capture it and let it loose outside."

"Capture it? With what? Our hands?"

"No." She tried not to grin at his squeamish look. "We need to find a container of some type to put it in, so we can get it outside."

The bedroom held nothing of use, so Skye hurried back into the main area of the cabin, her gaze quickly scanning the room.

Adam followed, running into the kitchen, yanking open cupboard doors and pulling out random drawers. "We got this. We're two intelligent adults. We can handle one fairly small, albeit repulsive, winged creature."

"Are you trying to convince me or yourself?"

He let out a nervous chuckle. "Both, I guess. I've never been in a situation like this. It's not something I see in my line of work. Any obstacle I face is on a computer screen in a video game. I would normally just look in my weapons arsenal and pull out a two-handed axe to use. Or a rocket launcher."

She laughed. "A rocket launcher might be a little over the top."

"Well, I'm not having any better luck in here." He shuffled through the utensil drawer and held up a spatula. "Not unless this would work."

She couldn't tell if he was being serious or not. "For what?

He's not a pancake."

"Right. I know that." He dropped the utensil back in the drawer and opened the utility closet. "How about a fire extinguisher? We could squirt him out of there."

"I applaud your inventiveness, but I don't think that's our best option."

"No? Okay, we'll keep it on the back burner for now. But it's an idea."

"Noted," she said, her head buried in the pantry as she rummaged through the scant offering of dishes. Spying a disposable clear plastic bowl, she grabbed it and held it up. "Found something."

"Yes, perfect," he declared, holding his arm out to let her walk ahead of him. "But I'm going to be a gentleman and let you try it first."

"Thanks. How chivalrous." She grabbed a magazine off the coffee table then crossed back to the bedroom, scanning the drapes first to make sure the bat hadn't already come out on its own.

"Is it still there?"

She jumped as Adam whispered close to her ear. She hadn't felt him come up behind her. "Holy crickets. You scared me." She arched an eyebrow at the spatula he must have grabbed back out of the drawer.

He offered her a sheepish grin. "Just in case."

"It's still there." She slowly approached the curtain, with the plastic bowl held out in front of her. She looked up at Adam. "You ready?"

"To get rabies? No."

"To capture it in this bowl."

"Will I have to turn in my man-card if I say no?"

A loud laugh burst from her, startling the bat. It spread its wings, flapping them a couple times before settling back. "No, you can keep your man-card. But don't worry. It's more scared of you than you are of it."

"That's what they always say about rattlesnakes, right before they bite you."

"It's not a rattler. I'd be a lot more nervous if we were trying to get a rattlesnake out of your bedroom."

His face paled. "Is that a possibility?" His voice carried a note of panic.

"No. I've never had to clear a rattlesnake from a guest cabin." She laughed again. "For the record, this is my first bat eradication, as well."

"You're not instilling me with a lot of confidence. I'm counting on you to be the wildlife expert here."

"All right, then, let's do this. You got your spatula ready?"

He held the pancake turner up like a sword, smiling. "Ready."

"That might actually be helpful. Once I get the bowl on it, you can use the spatula to scoop it in. I'll cover the bowl with this magazine."

"I'm with you."

She gripped the bowl but was surprised when he put his hand down on top of hers. "Be gentle," he said. "And go slow. Bats are pretty fragile, and we don't want to hurt it."

A feeling of warmth flowed through her, both from the heat of his hand and his thoughtfulness. He'd spent the last five minutes telling her how grossed out he was by the bat, but he was still worried about the animal getting hurt.

She took a deep breath then pressed the bowl to the curtain, trapping the bat inside. Holding the magazine ready, she nodded at Adam. "Okay, slide the spatula behind the bowl. Just keep it in there while I cover it."

He followed her instructions, grimacing as he gently slid the pancake turner between the curtain and the bowl. She pulled the bowl back slightly and pushed the magazine in from the other side.

The whole operation took about four seconds. Holding her hand over the magazine, she carried it outside, walking several yards into the forested hillside behind the cabin. "Bats have a hard time flying from the ground, so I'm going to put it on a tree."

"Good plan," he said, following a few steps behind her.

Finding a suitable tree, she pressed the bowl against the side then carefully pulled the magazine free. The bat inched forward then clung to the bark. She pulled the bowl away and took a step back. "The poor thing is probably traumatized."

Adam narrowed his eyes as he studied the bat clinging to the tree. "It's really not very big. You know the world's largest bat has a wingspan of up to six feet."

She let out a laugh and shook her head. "All right, Einstein. Let's leave this *little* bat alone and go back into the cabin."

Skye followed him back inside, then dropped onto the sofa in the main room. She offered Adam a weak grin. "Welcome to Hawk's Ridge Ranch."

He fell into the chair across from her. "Thanks. Do all of your guests get a wildlife adventure on their arrival?"

"Only the special ones." Her smile turned shy, and she could feel heat warming her neck. The *special* ones? "We usually charge extra for it, though."

He chuckled. "Put it on my tab. Or better yet, put it on Brandon's."

"The ranch will be picking up the tab for this one. Don't worry. I'll move you up to the lodge while we get the cabin cleaned up. It's almost a good thing that your friends didn't show up. I wouldn't know where to put all of you. I've only got one room left."

"Is the ranch full this week?"

"No. We're actually under capacity. But your group paid extra for some private excursions, so I didn't have to book as many people this week. That's giving me the chance to get some much needed repairs done on a few of the older cabins."

"I'm glad we could help, but I'm a little nervous about what kind of private excursions Brandon booked. Was this one of them? Did he pay extra to be met by a wild animal on our arrival?"

She arched an eyebrow at him. "If he did, he'd probably want his money back. That little guy wasn't much of a wild animal. But don't worry—we threw that one in for free."

He laughed, and the sound warmed her. She liked his laugh—liked him.

He was different than most of the men she knew. The guys around here were mostly country boys. They drove trucks and wore work boots and spent their days outdoors.

Adam didn't appear to have ever even been out in the country before, and whoever sold him those fancy snakeskin boots should be shot.

Maybe she was just lonely. Hawk's Ridge was set up in the mountains above the small town of Cotton Creek. Living on the ranch made for a fairly solitary life. Sure, she had a few friends in town, and she had Cody and Cal, and Clint, her neighbor to the south, but most of the people she saw were guests that popped in and out of her life for only one week.

But she didn't think loneliness was the problem. She was too busy to be lonely.

Besides, plenty of men had shown up at the ranch from time to time, plenty of good-looking single men. But none of them had made her face flush and her stomach do funny little flips when they laughed at one of her dumb jokes.

No, there was something about Adam. Something different.

He's still a guest, she reminded herself. And he was still going to leave in a week. So it didn't matter how cute he was or how his smile sent little shivers of heat coursing down her spine. She didn't do flings—she couldn't afford to. She didn't have the time or the energy to waste on trivial liaisons.

Speaking of affording, she'd been counting on the cost of those private excursions to help cover a few of her outstanding debts. She couldn't let Adam cancel them.

"The excursions are actually a lot of fun. You won't want to miss them. Brandon signed you up for the works: a cattle drive, an overnight camping trip on the ridge, as well as private horseback riding and lasso-throwing lessons. You should still do them. I was scheduled to be the instructor. With Brandon and Ryan not here, it looks like you'll get me all to yourself."

She cut her eyes to the fireplace, avoiding his gaze. *All to yourself?* What was wrong with her? Had she really just said that?

"I can't wait," he said, grinning.

Chapter Three

This is shaping up to be an interesting week.

"We should probably get your stuff and get you moved up to the lodge." Skye pushed off the sofa and reached for his bag.

"I've got it." Adam picked up his things and followed her from the cabin.

They chatted easily as they walked toward the lodge. "So, do you and your friends often go on vacation together?" she asked.

"Yes. No. Well, not really. We work together, and we've been friends since college, so we often travel together. But mostly it's for business—like scouting out locations for research. Still, we have a lot of fun. We met in college and went into business together in the field of computer engineering. They're great guys, my best friends. And the stuff we do in our business is super cool. I love going to work. Sometimes I can't believe I get paid to just hang out with my friends and do what I love."

"That does sound cool. Tell me about your business."

"Like I said, it's all computer related. But it's fun stuff. At least to us. We're working on a new project now—a new game. That's the main thing we do—we design and create video games."

She groaned.

"Uh-oh. What's wrong? You don't like video games?"

"It's not that. Honestly, I've never even played one. But I feel like they are the bane of my existence."

"Why?"

"You met my son earlier? The sulky twelve-year-old?"

He nodded.

"He didn't used to be like that. He used to be a sweet loving boy that wanted to hang out with me. Heck, he even liked to *talk* to me. Now, I barely recognize him. And I barely see him. He's always in his room, on his computer or that dang gaming system. That's all he wants to do. Ever. Play those stupid games."

He winced.

"Sorry. No offense."

"None taken. I understand. They are quite addicting." He shrugged. "It's good for our business, but evidently not so good for moms of teenage boys."

"I just don't get the appeal."

"Have you ever tried to play one?"

"No. I run this place practically by myself. I don't have time to spend on the computer, shooting aliens or stealing cars or whatever it is that happens in those games." This conversation had taken a wrong turn. She needed to change the subject and quit insulting his livelihood. "So, you said you were working on a new game. What's it about?"

"No aliens or car theft, I'm afraid. Most of our games are adventure-based. Our most popular series is called *Masters of Misfortune* and features the Fortune family. Victor, Gemma, and Theodore Fortune are siblings that travel through time, searching for ancient artifacts and amassing wealth. Each one is set in a different place and time period. Players have to complete missions or solve puzzles or fight off enemies to get to the ultimate goal. For instance, in one of our games, you traverse through a dangerous jungle in order to find a hidden treasure in a lost Mayan city. It's obviously more complicated than that, but that's the general idea."

"That actually sounds kind of fun."

"It is, I hope. Or at least, millions of gamers seem to think so."

Millions? She swallowed. Maybe she should have charged these guys more.

"What's the adventure of the new game?"

A smile tugged at the corner of his lips. Dang, but he had great lips. "This one is finding a buried treasure, too, but it's set back in the Old West. The Fortunes head back in time to the Wild West and search for a map that leads to a lost silver mine. One of the coolest things about what we do is that before we come up with a game, we always take a trip to wherever we're setting it. So, for our last game, we spent a week in the jungles of Peru, and a few weeks traveling around Europe touring ancient catacombs and mausoleums. Our second game was a pirate adventure. That one was a little harder to research. We couldn't exactly book passage on a pirate ship."

"No, I guess not."

"But we did find a guy down in Jamaica who let us spend a few days on his schooner. I'm not going to tell you that I got horribly seasick, but let's just say, that was an experience I don't need to have again."

"Oh no."

"Oh yes. Have you ever been on a big ship?"

She thought of the small row boat that her dad used to take out on the lake. "No. But I've been on a small boat. And I've rafted the Arkansas River. We're pretty land-locked here in Colorado. I've actually only seen the ocean once."

"Once? Really?"

"Really. Being a single mom and helping my dad with the ranch hasn't allowed me a lot of time for world travel."

"No, I guess not. I live in California, so I see the ocean every day. But I don't often get to see mountains like these." He stopped on the steps of the lodge and gestured to the scenery around them. "You don't need to travel when you get to live in a place like this."

She appreciated his sincerity. She loved the mountains. They were part of her soul—they were home.

"That's why we like to visit the places we're trying to create. So we can really get a sense of how they feel and smell and taste." His gaze fell to her lips when he said the word "taste," and a surge of heat swirled in her stomach.

She licked her lips, imagining for just a moment what his lips would taste like against hers. Then she caught herself. This was business, nothing more.

"Well, this place can feel dusty and gritty and can alternately smell like horses, pine trees, and cow manure. I don't know how you'd translate that into a video game."

"Thank goodness they haven't invented smell-o-vision," he said with a grimace.

She laughed. He still made her smile.

"It's the little nuances that help us bring the games to life. We really want an authentic western feel to this one, so Brandon suggested we come out here to research the idea, even though none of us have ever been to Colorado or have any experience with horses or cows."

"How about a bat?"

He chuckled. "Or a bat."

"I had no idea you'd never been to Colorado. I feel awful that you were welcomed by a critter flying around your room."

"Don't. Now that it's over, I think it's pretty cool. I can't wait to tell the guys about it. Although I may embellish my efforts a bit."

She grinned. "Your secret's safe with me."

"I think I'll use it, too. We can have the Fortunes get off the stagecoach and their first mission will be to fight off the rabid bat that's inhabiting their room at the saloon."

Her grin widened. "I like it." She led him through the lobby of the lodge, imagining how it looked through his eyes.

The dining room was off to the right. They served meals family-style at round oak tables with barrel-backed chairs, and a mason jar filled with fresh wild flowers sat in the center of each one. The flowers seemed cheery to her, but maybe the room seemed antiquated and dull to him.

The main room had a lofted ceiling, and a huge stone fireplace took over the back wall, the stonework rising all the way up. Plump leather couches and chairs surrounded the fireplace, grouped to encourage conversation.

Baskets of cinnamon pine cones sat on either side of the fireplace grate, their scent filling the room.

It was cozy, tempting a person to come in and sit a spell. She loved it. It was home to her. She'd grown up here, and memories of spending time with her father filled every room.

She usually showed off the lodge with a sense of pride, even bragging about the few celebrities who had hung their hats there. So why was she suddenly worried that some cute guy from California might judge it?

She snuck a glance at Adam.

He seemed to be looking around the room in wonder, a look of genuine delight on his face. He didn't appear to be judging it at all.

"What do you think? Of the lodge, I mean."

"I think it's awesome." He grinned at her, his expression similar to one of a kid in a candy store. "It's so authentic. And it smells amazing—like cinnamon and leather. This place is really cool."

A grin tugged at the corner of her lips. "Yeah, it is."

"Did your dad really build all of this for your mom?"

Her smile fell. "Yeah, he did. But she didn't appreciate it. They met when they were nineteen, and she was out here visiting her cousins for the summer. She was from the east coast and even though she thought she loved my dad, she didn't really take to country life." She shrugged. "Or family life. I guess she couldn't handle being up here alone, so she took off and left us when I was still in grade school. After that, it was just me and my dad."

"That must have been rough."

"It was." She shrugged. "But you can't change your past. You can only try to make the future better. And I'm sure my mother's leaving has influenced the kind of mom that I am. I'm probably a little too overprotective, but I'm also really committed to being around for my son. Even though I think Cody sometimes wishes I wouldn't."

"I think all kids pull away a little as they hit the teenage years."

"Yeah, probably. It's still hard. He's always looked up to me, and now he seems to think everything I say is dumb. He constantly reminds me that I have no idea what it's like growing up these days. As if I was never a teenager myself. And he hasn't even turned thirteen yet. I don't know how we're going to get through the next five years."

"You'll make it. Just the fact that you're worried about it tells me that you're a good mom."

"Thank you. I needed to hear that." Even if the guy barely knew her, it still helped to have someone, anyone, telling her she was doing a good job. She offered him a grateful smile.

They stopped at the reception desk, and she pulled a ring of keys from her pocket, selecting one to unlock a wooden box behind the counter. She took a key from the box then relocked it. "I'll put you in Room Four. It's on the main level, right down the hall from my living quarters."

Why did she just tell him that? She mentally shook her head. She definitely needed to get out more.

"You live *here*? In the lodge?"

"Yeah. My dad had a small apartment built onto one side of the building when I moved home with Cody. It's got its own kitchen and a couple of bedrooms. It makes it easier to take care of the guests since the lodge is the central building."

She led him down the hall to his room, unlocked the door, and then handed him the key. "I'll let you get settled. I wasn't expecting anyone to stay in this room, so I'll bring down some fresh towels and amenities when I get a chance."

He dropped his bag on the bed. "This is great."

She crossed the room and poked her head into the bathroom, then turned back to him with a grin. "All clear. No bats, snakes, or pesky varmints of any kind."

He chuckled. "Good to know."

"I'll let you relax. Don't forget, dinner's at six. We're serving fried chicken tonight, so you don't want to miss that."

"I wouldn't miss it for the world."

• • •

Adam sank onto the bed after Skye left.

Nope, wouldn't want to miss fried chicken night. Hopefully someone might bring out a banjo, and they could all have a sing-a-long after supper.

What had he gotten himself into?

At least the room in the lodge was nice and the bed seemed comfortable. Besides the queen-size bed, the room held a desk, a TV stand, and a brown overstuffed recliner tucked into the corner. The western touches were everywhere, from the Mason jar candles to the bedside lamp shaped like a bear.

If nothing else, he was getting plenty of material for the game. He'd have to take some notes later on some of his first impressions of the ranch, and give some thought as to how he could incorporate them into the game.

But his first impressions of Skye, he was keeping to himself. He couldn't quite put his finger on what it was that was so intriguing about her. He couldn't stop thinking about her—the way her hair smelled, the light splattering of freckles across her pert nose, the heat of her breath against his cheek, the way she looked up at him, her brown eyes soft and her lips slightly parted.

And the fact that he'd been tempted to lean down and kiss her.

What the hell was that all about? He did not do things like that. He was a planner. An engineer. He did things in a certain order, things that made sense.

And kissing Skye Hawkins didn't make any kind of sense at all.

Besides, she probably would have slapped him.

He didn't even know her.

Yet, he had this odd sense that he did. At least, they'd connected. Connected in that way that sometimes happens when you meet someone and instantly like them, knowing that you could easily be friends.

Except he didn't want to be friends with Skye. Well, not *just* friends.

Not unless their friendship allowed him to toss her onto the bed and strip her out of those tight-fitting jeans. Something he could not stop thinking about doing.

This woman was making him crazy.

He needed to focus on something else. Like how much his damn feet were killing him. And how much he wanted to get these stupid boots off.

Leaning down, he grabbed the heel of one boot and tried to pull his foot free.

The damn thing was stuck.

Shit. Now he'd have to wear these asinine boots the whole time he was here.

He pulled again, letting out a curse as a knock sounded at the door.

His heart raced. Damn, he had it bad for this girl. She'd only been gone for ten minutes, and he was already hoping it was her.

He wondered if it would be bad form to ask her to help him get these damn boots off.

"Come on in," he called.

A key jiggled in the lock, and the door swung open. But instead of Skye's smiling face, it was her broody preteen son who appeared. His arms were laden with fresh white towels and a stack of amenities.

"I brought you some towels," the kid mumbled. "Where do you want 'em?"

"You can put them on the bed." Adam suddenly had an idea. He nodded at his boot-encased foot. "Got any tips on how to get these off?"

A smirk crossed the boy's face. "Not by yanking on them. There should be a boot jack in the closet." He dropped the towels on the bed, crossed to the closet, and opened the door. Bending down, he grabbed a triangle-shaped device and handed it to Adam. "Here. Put your heel in the U-shaped part, then step on the back and pull your foot free. The jack holds the boot."

Adam dropped the device to the floor and followed the kid's instructions. In seconds, he was able to pull his foot out. He quickly did the other boot, then dropped down into the recliner and rubbed his sore arches.

"Thanks. It's Cody, right?"

The boy nodded.

"Thanks, Cody. I owe you, man."

"No problem. Where'd you get those boots anyway?"

"From some snake oil salesman in California," he muttered. The boy offered him an odd look, and Adam shrugged. "Some guy who saw a sucker walk into his store. He told me they were what everyone wore here in Colorado."

The kid looked down at the gray snakeskin-covered boots, then at his own square-toed leather ones. "I've never seen anyone wear anything like that."

Adam laughed. "Yeah, me neither. And now I'm stuck. I paid a hundred bucks for those stupid things, but I'd pay two hundred for a pair like yours, ones that were comfortable and didn't hurt like hell to walk in."

The boy cocked an eyebrow at him. "Two hundred bucks?"

Adam nodded.

"What size do you wear?"

"An eleven."

The boy stared at him for a few seconds, as if sizing him up, then crossed the room to the door. "I'll be right back," he said, then disappeared, leaving the door open a slight crack.

Chapter Four

Adam could hear the boy's boot heels hurrying down the hallway. He leaned back in the seat, stretching his legs out in front of him and flexing his toes.

Dropping his head back against the chair, he closed his eyes.

The door banged open a few minutes later, and Adam jolted at the sound. Blinking his eyes, he shook his head, trying to get his bearings. He must have actually fallen asleep.

This day had worn him out.

The kid barged in and dropped a large tan shoebox on the bed. The name "Justin" was printed on the side. Cody popped off the top and dug through the layer of tissue paper, then pulled a brown leather boot out.

The boot had a flat heel and the same square-toed design as the ones that Cody wore. The kid held the boot out. "These should feel much better."

Adam reached out to take the boot, but the boy pulled it back.

"You said something about two hundred dollars."

Adam chuckled. "Yes, I did." He pulled his wallet from his back pocket and freed two hundred dollar bills, then pitched them on the bed.

Cody tossed him the boot and pocketed the bills.

He ran his hand over the smooth leather. He could already tell these boots were going to be better. They even smelled different. Like real leather.

He pulled up his sock then stuffed his foot down into the boot, expecting the same harsh fit, but his foot slid easily into the boot. He sighed in relief.

He held out his hand for the other one. Cody passed it to him, and he put it on, then stood and walked back and forth across the room.

The boots fit perfectly. He offered Cody a thankful grin. "Thanks, kid. These are awesome. Well worth the price."

"You should just get rid of those other ones. Unless you like people making fun of you."

Adam laughed. This kid had some jokes. "I'll do that. Thanks again. I owe you one."

"No problem." He pointed to the sticker that cut diagonally across Adam's bag. "Why do you have that sticker?"

He'd ripped the side of his bag as he was trying to walk out the door that morning. Too late to change bags, he'd grabbed a *Masters of Misfortune* sticker from a stack of marketing material on his counter and slapped it across the tear. He figured it would hold long enough to keep the rip from getting bigger as the bag traveled through the airport.

"It's covering a hole in my bag. You familiar with the game?"

The kid let out a sarcastic laugh. "Uh, yeah. Everybody is."

"You play?"

"All the time. It's like my favorite game."

"Which version?"

He tilted his head to the side. "Um, all of them really. But I guess I probably like the pirate one the best."

"You get the new one yet?"

"The London one?"

Adam nodded.

"Yeah. I'm already on level twenty-nine."

"Nice work. The catacombs are cool, huh?"

Cody grinned. "Yeah. Wait, you play? *Masters of Misfortune*?"

"You could say that." He sat back down in the recliner. "What's your favorite part?"

"What do you mean?"

"Like what do you like about it? The game?"

"Um, everything. It's cool. I like the missions and the puzzles. That one part where you had to find your way out of the maze in Peru was pretty cool."

"Yeah, I liked that, too. But what is it about the actual game *play* that you like. And is there anything you don't like?"

Cody sat on the edge of the bed. He twisted his mouth to the side as he thought about it. "Well, there's one thing, but it's probably kind of stupid."

"I doubt it. You don't strike me as stupid. What is it?"

"It's Vic. You know, the main hero guy?"

"Yeah."

"I just wish he was more…" He paused as if searching for the right word. "Likeable, I guess."

"You don't like Victor?"

"Of course I like him, he's the main character. And he's the hero of the game. But it's just that sometimes he doesn't act like a hero. I mean, all he cares about is making money and finding the treasure. There isn't anything that's…just good about *him*, you know? Like, Gemma is the nice one—she cares about the people in the game—and Theo is the funny one. He makes everyone laugh. But all Vic ever talks about is the treasure."

Hmm. He'd never thought about it that way. "I see your point."

"The best heroes are guys you can look up to. They're always doing good stuff and acting heroic, like saving the town or something. But sometimes Vic just doesn't do anything." Cody shrugged. "Dumb, huh?"

"Not dumb at all. It's actually very smart. Really insightful. And it's something we're going to change."

"What do you mean 'we'?"

Adam narrowed his eyes at Cody. "You know when I said I'd played the game before?"

"Yeah."

"Well, I've actually played it a thousand times. Maybe a million, even. I've played every part of it because I helped create it. I'm one of the designers."

"No way. You work for Fishbowl Productions?"

He chuckled. "In a way. It's my company. Mine and my two buddies'. We started it after college. It's called Fishbowl Productions after the goldfish we had in our first apartment. Brandon is allergic to dogs and cats, so a fish was the only pet we could have."

Cody's eyes widened in disbelief. "What? I can't believe it. That's so cool, dude." His face fell and his expression changed to one of embarrassment. "Ah, crap. Sorry I just said all that stuff about Vic. I really do like your games. I play them all the time."

Adam held up a hand. "No, it's cool, really. I wanted to hear your honest opinion. That's why I didn't tell you I was one of the designers. And your ideas were really insightful. I totally intend to implement them in the next version."

"Thanks, man." The boy sat up taller on the bed. "There's more things that I love about the games. Like the mechanics are really good, compared to a lot of other adventure games on the market. The climbing and the jumping and the fighting all feel totally realistic."

Adam smiled. "That stuff is run by the physics engines. And those are what I design. I use real psychics to make it seem real, like when you're falling, you're actually accelerating at the correct rate, or when you throw a punch, the momentum is transferred in the right way."

"Or like when you jump, you don't fly ten feet in the air. Some games do that, and it just seems stupid."

"Exactly. That's all my work."

"Wow. Is it hard?"

"Sometimes. And sometimes, it's just time-consuming. It can take hours to create the simulation of throwing a simple rock. I have to make sure it falls in just the right arc or bounces a couple of times before it stops. But it's also pretty fun."

"That's really neat." A genuine smile covered his face, and Adam noticed his similarity to his mother. Not only was his smile the same, but Cody also had the same blond hair and sprinkling of freckles across his nose. He was just coming in to his height, and his body had that gangly, too-skinny look adolescents got.

It was good that he lived and worked on the ranch. It gave him a chance to get outside. That's probably how the kid stayed so lean. It couldn't be the fried chicken and gravy.

"So, do your friends play *Misfortune*, too?"

The boy's face fell, his smile gone. "What friends?"

Uh-oh. Sounded like he needed to tread carefully. "It's probably hard to hang out with buddies when the ranch is so far from town."

"It's practically impossible. Especially during the summer. During school, I have some friends I hang out with, but in the summer, no one wants to drive all the way up here. It sucks. I used to love the summer, but now I have to spend it working here so my mom doesn't lose this place. The only kids I see are usually stuck-up rich kids who are only at the ranch for a few days."

"I can see what you mean." Obviously this kid needed a friend. Even though he, too, would only be around for a few days, at least he could listen now. He remembered the painful days of adolescence all too well.

He'd also caught the part about Cody's mom needing his help so she didn't lose this place. Was Skye in financial trouble? The ranch seemed to be in good shape, but he had no idea how much it cost to run a place like this.

"What about that girl who showed up today? The one having a birthday?"

Cody looked down at his boots. "Who, Haylee?"

"Is that her name? She was pretty cute."

He shrugged. "I guess."

"Isn't she about your age?"

"Close. She just turned thirteen. And I'll be thirteen this fall. We're in the same grade."

"Any chance she's from around here?"

Cody shook his head. "Denver. It's not too bad, only about an hour away. Better than the last kid that I thought was kind of cool. He was from Den*mark*."

Adam chuckled. "That's quite a difference."

"But he still knew about *Misfortune*."

"Do you play with him online, then?"

"Sometimes. But it's kind of hard with the time difference. Mostly I play on my own."

"Let me know if you ever want to buddy up. I'll play on your team."

"How? Don't you already know how to do everything?"

"Most of it. But it's good for me to go in from a player perspective. It helps me pick out bugs and come up with ideas on how to tweak the next version. Plus, I still think it's fun."

The boy narrowed his eyes at him. "Are you serious?"

"Of course. My gamer tag is AtomAdam3.14. You can add me to your list. Do you play on a gaming system or on a PC?"

"Both. Mostly on my PlayStation."

"Okay. I'll watch for you, then I'll see if I can add some gold to your arsenal."

"That would be pretty cool. I'll get on tonight after supper and add you." He glanced at the bedside clock, as if the mention of supper had just reminded him of how late it was. "Crap. I gotta go. I'm supposed to be setting up in the dining room. See ya." He offered a small wave as he hurried from the room, pulling the door shut behind him.

Adam leaned back in the chair again and let out a sigh.

It appeared he'd just made a friend.

• • •

The smell of fried chicken filled the lodge as Adam made his way down to the dining hall. He couldn't remember the last time he'd had a home-cooked meal, and his mouth watered at the thought.

He'd been in such a hurry to leave for the airport, he'd missed lunch, and his stomach rumbled at the sight of the steaming bowls of potatoes, corn, and biscuits laid out on the tables.

"Hey, Adam," Cody said as he passed in front of him with a platter of fried chicken. "I think you're at the table on the right. Your name is on the little card in the middle."

"Thanks," he muttered to the boy's back. Cody had already set the plate on a table and was heading back toward the kitchen.

Adam maneuvered his way through the chairs, weaving his way toward his table.

The honeymooners were already there, and he sat in one of the three empty chairs. He assumed the other two seats were for Brandon and Ryan.

He nodded at the couple. "Hi, I'm Adam. We rode in on the bus together."

"Yeah, nice to meet you." The guy stood slightly from his chair and held out a hand. "I'm Josh, and this is my wife, Brittany." He grinned. "I can't get used to saying that. We just got married yesterday."

"Congratulations." He picked up his napkin and folded it across his lap, then looked awkwardly around the room. He hated small talk.

"Thanks," Josh said. "We're pretty excited."

His new wife didn't look excited at all. She stared glumly into her glass of tea, as if the answers to life might be floating amongst the ice cubes.

But the guy had a goofy smile on his face. It was obvious he wanted to chat.

"We're from Denver," Josh continued. "Although we've been living in Fort Collins. We just graduated from Colorado State."

"But Josh can't find a job," Brittany chimed in, her voice monotone as she continued to stare at her glass. "So we've moved into his parents' basement. That's also why we're celebrating our honeymoon at a dude ranch less than an hour from our house instead of on a beach in Mexico."

Adam might not be the most intuitive guy when it came to understanding women, but he sensed some obvious hostility coming off of this one.

Josh shrugged. "I keep trying to tell her that people come from all over the country to go to this place. Just because it's in our home state doesn't mean it's not a great vacation spot."

Adam had to agree with Brittany. He'd also prefer to be at the beach, soaking up the sun with a cold beer in his hand, but he didn't say anything. It seemed like the poor guy already had his hands full with his sulky bride.

Time to change the subject. "What did you get your degree in?" he asked.

"Parks and Rec Administration. I love nature and like working with kids. My dad was pushing me to go into business, but I wanted to go into a field I would actually enjoy. Unfortunately, a lot of people have the same idea. The job market is pretty saturated. But I'll find something. It's just a matter of time. I think the perfect job is right around the corner."

"Well, good luck." He really meant it. The guy seemed earnest enough, and he obviously believed the perfect job was just around the corner. More power to him.

Skye slid into the seat next to him, and his heart rate increased. He wiped his suddenly damp palms on his napkin.

"Is it all right if I sit here?" she asked, smiling first at him and then at the honeymooners. "I figured your table would be a little light without your coworkers."

Her smile was sending funny darts of heat along his spine. And he could smell her perfume, or her shampoo, or her skin. Something apple mixed with the scent of vanilla and some kind of flowers wafted around her, and his head swam with the intoxicating scent.

"Yeah, of course you can sit with us."

"Thanks." Skye offered him a grin, then turned to the other two at the table. "Hi there. You must be Josh and Brittany, right?"

Oh brother. He hated small talk enough the first time around—now he was going to have to hear it again.

"They're from Denver, recent college grads, he can't find a job, and she's pissed 'cause they're living in his parents' basement and not at the beach."

"Oh," Skye said, looking from Adam to Josh.

Brittany's gaze was still on her ice cubes, but she did offer an eye roll and an impressive sigh.

Oh shit. Did he just say that out loud?

Chapter Five

Adam grimaced. "Sorry. Remember earlier when I told you I can sometimes be an asshole." He hazarded a glance at Josh. "Sorry, didn't mean to sound like a jerk."

The younger man shrugged and let out an awkward chuckle. "It's cool. You pretty much summed things up."

"It's nice to meet you both," Skye said, offering the couple an encouraging smile. "And if it helps, Brittany, I'd rather be at the beach right now, too."

Oh man. A sudden image of Skye in a bikini—half naked and covered in tanning oil—filled his head, and he felt heat in places other than just his spine.

"Adam? Hello? Earth to Adam."

He blinked, shaking his head as he realized that Skye had just asked him a question. And it hadn't been about rubbing oil on her back. "Sorry. What?"

"I asked if you would mind passing the chicken." She narrowed her eyes at him. "You okay?"

"Yeah. I'm okay." He was an idiot, but he was okay. He picked up the platter of fried chicken and passed it around the table.

They settled into more small talk, which mostly consisted of Skye asking questions, Josh offering animated answers, Adam listening, and Brittany sulkily gnawing on the end of a chicken leg.

He liked to listen to Skye talk. She was smart and insightful. And funny. He found himself smiling at her silly jokes and nodding as she offered sage wisdom to the newlyweds, even though he wasn't sure what he was agreeing with. He had no insight whatsoever when it came to relationships. Except what not to do.

Or what it felt like to get dumped. He could offer plenty of insight into that.

He didn't have a hard time getting dates, when he had the time and inclination to want to date, which wasn't all that often, since he seemed to work all the time. But women seemed to be interested in him, or at least interested in dating a guy that had money and drove a nice car. But they didn't seem as interested once they realized his work came first—always.

Apparently, being a workaholic did not make him very good boyfriend material. At least, according to the last three women who had broken up with him.

But none of those three women made his stomach twist and his palms itch the way that Skye did. Hell, even just thinking about her made his pulse quicken.

And he'd never had the kind of deliciously dirty thoughts about them like he'd had about Skye as he watched her eat a piece of cherry cobbler. There was something about the way her lips closed around the fork and the way her tongue slid across her upper lip to catch a stray bit of red cherry juice that was driving him crazy.

What the hell was wrong with him? He'd never gotten turned on by watching a woman eat before.

But he'd watch Skye do just about anything—eat, drink, shower.

"You certainly have a mischievous look on your face, Mr. Clark," Skye said, leaning toward him as she lowered her voice. "What are you thinking about?"

Heat rushed to his neck. *Busted.* "Um...well...you, I guess."

The corners of her lips tugged up in a grin. "Me? What were you thinking that could put that kind of smile on your face?"

Oh shit. He scrambled for something plausible to say—he couldn't very well tell her he'd been imagining her in the shower. "I was just thinking about how good you are with people."

Her grin broadened. "Thank you."

That hole to swallow him up could arrive any minute now. He needed to just make a graceful exit and go to his room.

He pushed back his chair, and it made a loud scrape on the hardware floor. "Thanks for dinner. It was delicious."

And thanks for letting me watch you eat your dessert.

His move must have given the rest of the room permission to leave, because several others pushed back their chairs, as well, and readied to leave.

Skye stood up next to him. "I think you're signed up for lasso lessons at nine. I guess I'll see you then."

Lasso lessons? He was seriously going to kill Brandon. "That sounds great. Thanks again." Out of habit, he held out his hand to shake hers, and then realized how awkward it seemed. But it was too late to pull it back.

She looked at his offered hand, then grinned up at him. "You are absolutely welcome." She slipped her hand into his and gave it a firm squeeze.

Fireworks shot off in his stomach. Maybe offering to shake hadn't been such a dumb idea—at least he got to touch her.

"Hey, nice boots," she said, glancing down at his feet. "What happened to the snake skins?"

He shook his head. "I know. Those boots were stupid. I was a sucker for buying them. Thank goodness for Cody."

"Cody?"

"Yeah. He set me straight earlier when he dropped those towels by my room. I actually had a lot of fun talking to him. He plays some of the games my company has created, and we had a good time discussing the merits and some of the failings of the game."

"Failings? He told you what was wrong with it? I swear I did try to teach that boy some manners."

He chuckled. "He has great manners. I asked him for his opinion, and I wanted an honest answer, so I didn't tell him they were our games until after he'd told me his thoughts. Besides, he had some good insight. I'm actually going to take his advice."

Her eyes widened. "Really?"

"Yeah. Really. He's a smart kid." He tipped up the toe of his boot. "And I owe him one for saving me with these boots. They're a thousand times more comfortable than those idiotic ones I brought with me. Best two hundred bucks I've ever spent."

"Two hundred bucks?" She raised an eyebrow at him. "You paid Cody two hundred dollars for those boots?"

"Yes. I offered two hundred, then he took off and showed up ten minutes later with a shoebox. Any chance you're surprised because I got such a great deal?"

"You got a great something, all right. And he's going to get a little something, too. We have a small gift shop here where we sell western knick-knacks, a few hats, moccasins, and some shirts and boots. We sell the ones you're wearing for around a hundred dollars. My son evidently charged you an extra one hundred dollar delivery fee to carry those boots about five hundred yards."

Adam shook his head, a grin pulling at his lips. He'd been taken by a twelve-year-old con artist, but he also had to admire the kid a little. It was a pretty ballsy move. "That little sneak."

"Yeah," Skye said, her expression not looking quite as amused as him. "That's just what I was thinking."

• • •

A few hours later, Adam was in his room, sprawled in the recliner as he turned the pages of the new psychological thriller he'd picked up in the airport. He'd changed into a pair of loose-fitting shorts and a T-shirt that read: *If God didn't create it—an Engineer did.*

A huge fan of the author, he was engrossed in the book, totally immersed in the gritty, dark world of suspense. He was just at the part where the sinister villain had chased his victim into a shadowy maze of tunnels under the city, complete with slime, rats, and most likely snakes, when a knock sounded on his door.

He jolted, the paperback flying from his hands.

"Adam?"

Holy crap. It was Skye.

He shook his head. What the hell was she doing here? It was close to ten o'clock. His heart pounded against his chest as he imagined her on the other side of the door, wearing just a western shirt and a pair of cowboy boots.

He huffed a quick breath in his hand and sniffed. Would it be weird to grab a mint? Did he have time to gargle a quick swig of mouthwash?

"Just a second," he called, glancing around the room to make sure nothing embarrassing was lying out. He'd emptied his pockets earlier and tossed the contents and his clothes onto the bed. Grabbing the packet of mints, he poured a couple into his mouth and crunched them with his teeth as he crossed the room then opened the door.

Skye was standing there—but she was not wearing his imagined wardrobe choice. In fact, she was wearing a frown as she marched a sullen Cody into the room.

He was wearing a similar expression.

"Hey, Adam. Sorry to bother you so late. But I had to wait until Cody got back from the campfire stories tonight. I believe he has something he wants to say to you. And something to give you."

Cody sheepishly held out the two wrinkled hundred dollar bills Adam had given him earlier. "Sorry."

"Wow," Skye said, sounding unimpressed. "That was really heartfelt. It almost brought a tear to my eye. Why don't you try again?"

He let out a long sigh, then looked up at Adam. "I'm sorry I tricked you out of this money. I should have been honest and told you the real price of the boots. Here's your two hundred dollars back. As a punishment for my dishonesty, I'm going to pay for the boots myself out of my ranch paycheck."

"That won't be necessary. I can certainly pay for them myself." Adam had a feeling this punishment would put a hardship on Skye as well as Cody.

"He can pay for them," Skye said.

"Listen, I don't want the profits of the store to suffer from a misunderstanding. I understand that Cody needs to take responsibility for his actions, so how about if I pay for the boots and then we work out another type of punishment that won't cause a problem with the ranch's finances."

"What kind of punishment?" Cody asked, his eyebrows wrinkled in skepticism.

"I'd really like him to work to pay off the boots," Skye

repeated.

"Okay. How about if he works for me? I'm really interested in his perspective on the *Misfortune* series. How about he writes up a report giving me insight into what he thinks I could do with the game?"

"Hmmm. I do like the idea of him writing a report."

"And maybe he could give me a tour of the ranch, and we could run through some live scenarios of things I was thinking we could do in the game."

Cody's eyes widened. "You want me to shoot some stuff? That would be cool."

"No shooting," Skye said.

"No. No shooting. But we were thinking about a horse chase and a wagon ride. He could probably offer a little guidance on both of those. And it really would help me."

Skye looked from Cody to Adam, her face still registering skepticism. "I don't know."

"Look, I get that he shouldn't have taken the tip, but he did actually help me by pointing out my poor taste in footwear and setting me up with some boots that I can actually wear. Boots that are comfortable and hopefully don't make me look like as much of a dumbass as those snakeskin ones did." He winced. "Sorry. Anyway, I think he should get a little credit for making a sale for the store and offering great customer service by delivering my purchase right to my room."

"Yeah, Mom. He makes a good point. I did make some money for the shop and gave him some helpful advice on how to avoid looking like an idiot."

Skye arched an eyebrow at him, then held up her hand. "All right. You two have convinced me. I still don't think the helpful advice and delivery charge was worth a hundred dollars, but I'll let Adam keep the boots and pay for them. And I'll let Cody work off the hundred dollars by writing the report and spending two hours tomorrow helping you with the game. Does this seem feasible to everyone?"

He and Cody both nodded.

"Can I go now?" Cody asked, shifting from one foot to the other.

"Fine."

The boy offered Adam a quick wave as he hurried out the door.

"Here." Adam held out the money. "I really do insist on paying for the boots myself."

Skye took one of the hundreds and shoved it into the front pocket of her jeans. "Thank you. That's very nice. And thank you for being so understanding. I can't believe my son tried to cheat you."

He chuckled. "Honestly, I kind of admire the kid for it." He shrugged as Skye narrowed her eyes at him. "I do. He saw an opportunity to make a buck, and he took it. And seriously, I was happy to pay two hundred dollars to have a better pair of boots to wear. I don't mind spending money to get good quality. I like to wear stuff that holds up and that will last a long time."

Skye's eyes brightened and her voice took on a teasing note. "Yeah? Like that T-shirt?"

He grinned. "Hey. Don't be giving my shirt a hard time. I won this in an engineering competition in college. This came with a sweet trophy and a five-hundred-dollar scholarship."

"Did you need a scholarship?"

"You bet I did. I told you I was raised by a single mom, just like Cody. We didn't have a lot, but my mom always made sure my brother and I had what we needed. I have a lot of respect for women who raise kids on their own. I don't know how you do it."

Skye looked up at him, not saying anything as she blinked back the tears welling in her eyes.

Shit. He hadn't meant to make her cry.

He glanced around the room, anywhere but at her, at those gorgeous brown eyes that held enough pain to make his own chest hurt. He cleared his throat. "Sorry, didn't mean to make you upset."

"You didn't make me upset. Your words just touched me. Especially because I believe you really mean them."

"Of course I do. Why else would I say them? Life's too short, and I'm way too busy to waste time on inconsequential bullshit."

She laughed out loud, not like a small chuckle, but a full belly laugh. "I like you, Adam Clark. And I believe you may have just given me a new mantra." She pressed a hand to her stomach and offered him a flirty grin. "You are a dangerous combination. Cute *and* smart. And you smell nice. Minty."

A smile tugged at the corner of his lips.

"This is shaping up to be an interesting week," she said as she pulled open the door to his room. "Good night, Adam. I'll see you at breakfast."

He followed her to the door, searching for the right words to ask her to stay a little longer. But nothing seemed right. The dude ranch didn't have a bar, so he couldn't ask her for a drink, and they'd already had dinner together, in a sense.

"Good night, Skye." He leaned against the door jamb and watched her walk down the hall toward her room, letting out a chuckle as he heard her mutter the words "inconsequential bullshit."

• • •

The next morning, Skye sat at her desk, trying to make a dent in her mountain of paperwork before she started the business of her day.

A stack of unpaid bills lay scattered in front of her, and she leaned her forehead against her palm and let out a long sigh.

Tourism had been down the past few years, so between that and a few major repairs to the ranch this year, like an electrical fire in one of the cabins and the ranch truck breaking down, the expenses now outweighed the revenue.

Having Adam's company book the extra excursions would help to cover the electric bill this month, but she was still coming up short on several of the others.

She could only rob Peter to pay Paul so many times. Eventually Pete went broke, too.

She just needed to make it through the rest of the summer. Then she'd need to think of something big to generate new business.

A knock sounded on the door to her office, and she looked up to see a tall good-looking cowboy leaning against the door jamb.

He offered her a grin. "Now that's what I like to see—a woman who's not only beautiful, but also smart."

Chapter Six

Skye held in a groan. Of all the things she *did* need right now, a flirty cowboy wasn't even on her list. That wasn't fair. Clint Carson was her neighbor and one of her oldest friends. And as much as she hated to admit it, she did need the cowboy whose ranch lay next to hers.

He jerked a thumb behind him. "I saw Cody on the way out, and he let me in."

She pasted on a smile. "Hey, Clint. I wasn't expecting you till later this afternoon."

"I finished early and thought I'd stop in to see if you needed me for anything this morning."

The double-entendre was not lost on her, and her stomach clenched at the thought. She knew what he wanted from her, but she didn't have it in her to give it to him.

Clint was drop-dead gorgeous and had always been a perfect gentleman, filling in at the ranch and always there when she needed him. They'd been friends since they were kids. But Clint had been making it clear he wanted more than just their casual friendship. A lot more.

And really, it would be so easy. He was funny and nice and charming as heck, and they got along well. It would be so simple to let him step in and take care of her and Cody. The only problem was that she didn't feel a single ounce of attraction to him.

"Whatcha working on? Do you need a hand?" He took a step closer, his gaze roaming across the bills strewn across the desk.

Skye hastily pushed them under the keyboard, but she knew he'd already seen them—the words "Past Due" stamped in bright red against the white envelopes. "Nope. I think I'm all set. Just finishing up a few things here in the office."

"Looks like you're a little behind there."

Thanks, Captain Obvious, for pointing that out.

She was on a terror today. The past due bills were enough to make her crabby, but she'd also gotten into an argument with Cody that morning. He'd told her that he wanted to take the teenage daughter of one of the guests on a horseback ride that afternoon, just the two of them, and she'd told him no.

Apparently that made her the Wicked Bitch of the West.

He'd informed her that she had to let him grow up at some point and then he'd left the apartment, slamming the door behind him.

But none of that was Clint's fault. The guy was just being nice, and it wasn't fair to take her troubles out on him.

"I'll be fine," she said, trying for a lighthearted tone. "You know how everything picks up in the summer. That stupid electrical fire this spring didn't do me any favors, though."

"I could help, ya know. Give you a loan, just to get you through the season."

"No, really. Thank you, but I couldn't accept that." The last thing she needed to add to her mess of problems was being in debt to Clint Carson.

She didn't want to be in debt to anyone. And she sure as

hell wouldn't accept charity. She could, and would, do this on her own.

The ranch was her responsibility, and she wouldn't let her dad down, God rest his soul. He'd been gone for five years now, yet she still felt like she was trying to prove something to him—to show him that she could manage on her own. That just because she made one mistake twelve years ago, she wasn't a total dumbass.

Hawk had been friends with Clint's dad, who'd passed the good old boy mentality down to Clint. She hated the thought that he saw her as a weak woman who needed a man to step in and bail her out.

"You know you're not alone. You can count on me for whatever you need," he said.

Ugh. Now she felt even guiltier. Because the truth was that Clint *was* one of the good guys. He was genuinely nice and had never been anything but kind to her. And she *could* count on him. He'd been there for her after her dad died, helping with the details and making arrangements, when she couldn't even string two coherent thoughts together.

He dropped his hands onto her shoulders and massaged the tightness there. It should have felt good, having warm hands knead the sore muscles, but instead she fought against another wave of guilt. He seemed to always go out of his way to help her, and even though he didn't push her, he made it clear that he was interested and willing to take things to the next level.

He was a great catch, and someday he would make a very good husband for some woman. That woman just wasn't going to be her.

Sometimes she chastised herself for not even trying to make things work with him, but even now, with his big hands caressing her shoulders, she felt nothing more than friendship.

And really, she did value his friendship. Their land shared

water rights, and their fathers had been not just friends, but good neighbors, often helping each other out on the adjacent ranches. Both of their dads had often joked about her and Clint getting married and joining the family's lands.

But Clint didn't see it as a joke.

And he didn't seem to listen no matter how many times she told him she wasn't interested in getting married.

Not to him. Or anyone.

She had enough on her plate, trying to raise Cody and get the ranch out of the red. Having a man in her life right now would only complicate things.

Especially if that man was her exact opposite and lived in California.

Where had that come from?

She'd been thinking about Clint, not Adam. Yeah, right. Who was she kidding? She'd been thinking about Adam all morning. And all last night.

She couldn't seem to get the cute computer engineer out of her head. He'd looked so adorable the night before, in his glasses and funny T-shirt. But the thoughts she'd been having about stripping him of both his glasses and his shirt had been downright dirty.

"Come on, Skye," Clint said, breaking into her thoughts. "You know Hawk would hate to see anything happen to this place. We could work out a deal that would be mutually beneficial to both of us."

His hand slid across her shoulders and intimately caressed her neck. She clamped her hand down on his, stopping him from going any further, as annoyance filled her. It bugged the crap out of her when he used the memory of her father against her.

She took a deep breath, swallowing her irritation as she gave his hand a friendly pat, then pulled free of his grasp. "I know you're just trying to help, Clint. But I've got this. The ranch is my responsibility, and I'll take care of it. Besides, I've got some ideas about how to bring in some fresh revenue."

He narrowed his eyes at her, a frown forming on his face. "What kind of ideas?"

"I'm not ready to talk about them yet. They're still in the planning stages. But I'll let you know." *Yeah, I'll let you know as soon as I come up with some.*

She gestured to the door. "We should probably get outside. I think Cody is starting those lasso lessons, and there is a young newlywed couple that was interested in a private horseback ride. As long as you're here, do you think you could get them set up for that?"

He sighed, as if resigned about his advances being put off again. "Yeah, sure. Then I'll be back later this afternoon to help with supper and do the wagon ride."

"Sounds good."

Clint took on a few of the highlights that the ranch offered, taking the guests on an evening wagon ride, doing guided horseback tours, and helping with the country dance lessons.

He *was* a good guy, but he wasn't doing everything out of the goodness of his heart. They'd worked out a bartering system, where he helped her out with the ranch activities and she let him use a section of her land to graze his cattle. Plus, he got to keep the tips the guests offered, and with his wholesome, good looks and flirtatious grin, he often had the guests eating out of his hand. His cowboy charm, country twang, and western songs, helped ensure the guests had a great time.

And with the mountain of debt piling up around her, she needed her guests to have a good time—to tell their friends and to come back again.

So for now, whether she liked it or not, that meant she needed Clint.

• • •

Adam had spent the morning learning how to throw a lasso and discovering the fine art of how to muck out a stall, and his whole body ached. There wasn't anything in him that was remotely interested in learning how to dance the Texas Two-Step.

Taking a tentative step toward the door, he wondered if it would be bad form to duck out quickly before the lesson started. No one would probably even notice.

He risked a quick glance at Skye, and she flashed him a dazzling smile.

Shit. He wasn't going anywhere.

Not just because her smile did funny things to his insides, but because he didn't want to disappoint her. And it had been a long time since he'd really worried about disappointing a woman. Usually if his behavior bothered the woman he was dating, he considered it her problem, not his.

Which probably contributed to the reason he was still single.

But Skye was different. He wanted to please her, to make her happy, to earn that grin she'd just offered him so easily.

He listened with half an ear as Skye explained the steps, then she and her ranch hand, Cal, demonstrated them, first slowly, then in time with the music. They made the steps look effortless. The older man had a surprisingly strong sense of rhythm.

Dancing had never been something Adam excelled at, mainly because, unlike Cal, rhythm was one thing he was sorely lacking.

Standing on the edge of the dance floor brought back painful memories of uncomfortable school dances when he and his friends would convince each other to go, then hang around, praying that a girl would ask them to dance and hoping they wouldn't have to ever dance at all.

What made matters worse this afternoon was that he and the teenage girl Haylee were the only solo dancers. He knew eventually they were going to have to pair up to dance with someone. Talk about awkward.

"Now we'll all practice. Don't be shy. Grab a partner and circle around the middle of the dance floor," Skye instructed.

Crap. Here it came. The moment where he wished he could blend into the wall behind him. He knew he was being ridiculous. He could stand in front of a huge group of his employees for an hour, instructing them about how to use physics in their work, but a minute and a half on the side of a dance floor and his heart was pounding like a hammer against his chest.

Because this wasn't physics or science, where everything made sense and had a logical explanation. This was dealing with people and nerves. He could handle equations, but he didn't know how to fix not having rhythm.

"Adam, will you help me out and be my partner?" Skye asked, crossing the dance floor and holding out her hand.

Relief flooded him, and he offered her a smile, trying to play it cool and not show how relieved he was to be asked, and to not have to partner with the thirteen-year-old. He wiped his sweaty hand on his jeans before reaching out and taking hers.

He caught his breath as Skye stepped into his arms, fitting against him like two pieces of a puzzle. She rested her hand on his shoulder, and he felt the heat of her palm through the fabric of his shirt.

Resting his hand on her waist, he resisted sliding his hand along the lush curve of her hip. She took his other hand, holding it at shoulder height, then she tilted her face up to his and offered him an encouraging grin.

"You ready?"

"To make a fool of myself?"

"You're not going to make a fool of yourself. Most of the people here are new to this type of dancing."

"I'm new to any type of dancing. I can't even keep up with that stupid dance video game. Cal's the pro. He looks like Fred Astaire, and I'm more like Fred Flintstone."

She chuckled and gave him a flirty grin. "Maybe you've just never had the right partner. Dancing doesn't have to be hard. You just have to relax and let yourself *feel* the music." She slid a little closer to him, their bodies now mere millimeters apart.

He could feel something all right. But it wasn't the music. It was the closeness of her hips swaying next to his, the press of her thigh against his, with only a faded layer of denim between them. If she kept moving like that, she was going to feel something, too.

Awesome. Nothing like a mid-afternoon boner to let a girl know how you really feel.

Baseball. Think about baseball. Or physics. Or anything besides the curvy cowgirl that slowly led him around the dance floor.

He glanced around the room, trying to run a math calculation in his head.

No one was paying any attention to them. They were all focused on their own feet and counting the steps.

It looked like Cody had lucked out, too, filling in as the dance partner for the teen girl. Adam hoped he wasn't wearing the same goofy grin that the kid had on his face.

Although he didn't really care if he looked stupid. Despite the threat of a meddlesome hard-on, holding Skye in his arms felt like heaven. At least for him.

It probably wasn't so great for her, especially since he'd just stepped on her foot for about the fourth time.

He wasn't used to wearing boots, and when he added in

the effort of trying to learn the steps and keep in time with the music, he was pretty much a dancing disaster.

Thankfully Skye was a patient teacher, counting out the steps and guiding him around the floor with one hand on his shoulder and the other clasped tightly in his.

Her cinnamon-scented breath tickled his ear as she softly directed the steps. “Quick, quick, slow, slow.”

“You’re good at this,” he told her, his eyes trained on their feet.

“You’ll get the hang of it, too. It just takes practice,” she said, reaching over and tilting his chin back up to look at her. “I’m sure I couldn’t walk into your office and start doing computer stuff or whatever it is you do. But the more you do it, the better you’ll get.”

Right. He shouldn’t expect to be a pro at this, even though he was good at most everything else that he tried. Well, everything that involved using his brain.

“Computer stuff is easy. Dancing is complicated, especially with the distraction of having a beautiful woman pressed against me.”

Oh shit. What the hell had happened to his filter?

She raised an eyebrow at him, a grin tugging up the curve of her lips.

He held his breath, then let it out, his own smile curving his lips as she pressed a little closer to him, lining her hips nearer to his and pressing her breasts against his chest.

Tightening his grip on her hand, he tried to relax his shoulders, to feel the music.

But he kept getting distracted by the smell of her hair and the way her lips parted as she whispered the words, “Quick, quick, slow, slow.” He knew she was talking about their feet, but he kept imagining her whispering “slow, slow” into his ear as he nuzzled her neck or laid down next to her.

Her cheek grazed his, her voice soft as she spoke next to

his ear. "Relax. You're doing great. Bend your knees a little." Her leg slid easily between his, her thigh pressed against his as she led him with her body.

Heat surged through his veins, and he slid his hand a little farther around her waist.

She lowered their joined hands and pressed them to his waist, guiding his hips with their hands.

Glancing down at her, his mouth went dry as she smiled up at him. Her gaze flicked to his lips. Just for a moment, but he'd caught it, and fire swirled in his belly.

Leaning in, just a little closer, he was caught up in the moment—the slow rhythm of the music, the sway of their hips as they glided across the floor, the brush of her soft hair against his arm, the temptation to press his lips to hers.

The rest of the room faded away as he leaned closer, as if pulled by an invisible string, so tempted to kiss her.

Her lips parted slightly, and he heard the quick hitch in her breath.

"Hey, Skye. Are we doing this right?" a voice called from across the room, breaking the spell.

His steps faltered as he came to his senses, remembering that they were actually in a room full of people.

Skye pulled back, glancing toward one of the couples in the class and offering them a smile of encouragement. "Yes, you've got it. Bend your knees, though. Stay loose."

She looked back up at him, an impish grin covering her face. "You ready for the next step?"

He swallowed. "The next step?"

"Yep. You ready to try a turn?"

He chuckled. "Yeah, I'm ready to try anything." His lips curved into what he hoped was an irresistible grin.

She laughed, spinning him around, and the sound of her laughter trickled down his spine like warm oil.

Her enthusiasm was contagious, and after a few songs, he

started to relax and get the hang of the steps, even attempting a dip. He was feeling pretty good—he wouldn't go so far as to say confident, but he was more relaxed and actually having fun.

Then Captain Cowboy sauntered into the barn.

You would have thought Sam Elliott himself had just walked in the door, the way the women in the group practically swooned over the guy.

The cowboy worked the room, grinning and complimenting the women on their steps as the song wound down.

The music stopped, and Skye dropped his hand and took a step back. The other man walked up to them, ignoring Adam, and gave Skye a broad smile. "Hey, darlin'."

Was this guy for real?

"Hey, Clint," Skye answered, then gestured to Adam. "This is Adam Clark, from California. He's one of the guests here. Adam, this is Clint Carson, my neighbor and my good friend. We practically grew up together."

Clint Carson? Seriously? The guy even had a cool cowboy name.

The man took his hand, applying a little more pressure than necessary and holding on just a beat too long.

Point taken.

"Pleased to meet ya." He grinned at Adam, but his smile didn't quite reach his eyes, and he took just the smallest step forward, just enough to position himself between Adam and Skye. "What do you do in California, Adam?"

"Adam designs video games," Skye answered.

Well, he did a little more than that, but he didn't want to contradict Skye. He didn't have anything to prove to this guy. Did he?

"That sounds fun. Wish I could play games for a living." Clint smiled good-naturedly, but Adam still felt the smallest wave of condescension coming off of him.

He turned back to Skye, effectively dismissing Adam. "Sorry, I'm late. I had a mare that threw a shoe, and I had to wait for the farrier."

"Oh shoot. She wasn't hurt, was she?"

"Nah. We think she did it on the trails. They were up working by the stream, and it was pretty boggy. But she's fine."

What the heck were they talking about? It was like they had their own language.

Although people could probably say the same about him and Brandon and Ryan when they started talking about server architecture, batch scripts, and other programming jargon.

"Sorry I'm late, folks," Clint said loudly, addressing the other couples in the room. "It looks like you're doing great with the Two-Step. How about if we move on and teach you a little Country Swing?" He tipped his cowboy hat and flashed a charming smile.

The room tittered in agreement, and Skye crossed to the CD player to set up a different series of songs.

Clint offered Adam a conspiratorial wink. "Thanks for filling in, but I've got it from here." He sauntered after Skye, joking around with the room as he explained the first few steps. Within minutes he had the group eating out of his hand.

Adam's teeth ground together. Something about this guy irritated the hell out of him. He tried to tell himself it wasn't just the familiar way he had with Skye, easily touching her shoulder and wrapping his arm around her waist to demonstrate a step.

No, it felt like something more, something just under the surface.

But obviously Skye didn't feel that way as she laughed with him, putting on a show for the guests.

He tapped his fingers against his leg and told himself to unclench his jaw. But his teeth remained clamped together as the next song started, the beat picked up, and Clint grabbed Skye, pulling her into his arms and gliding her around the dance floor, moving easily from the Two-Step into some sort of swinging, twisting, swirling dance.

Uncrossing his arms, he tried to keep from scowling as he once again stood on the sidelines, watching the cool guy dance with the pretty girl.

They made the perfect pair, their steps in exact rhythm, their pacing fluid and familiar as they progressed through the song, as if they'd danced together a hundred times before.

And they probably had.

A hard rock formed in his chest as he watched them. Skye seemed to fit perfectly into Clint's arms, reminding Adam that a guy like him had no chance in hell at winning this girl.

All the fantasizing he'd been doing about her had been just that—a fantasy.

He slipped out of the dance lessons and trudged toward the lodge.

• • •

The tape measure slid shut, and Adam jotted the measurement of the fence post in his notebook. He'd tried to stay in his room after the dance lesson fiasco, but the walls felt like they were closing in on him.

He'd purchased a small spiral notebook from the gift shop and had spent the last few hours wandering around the ranch, taking pictures and measurements of different objects as part of his research for the new game.

He tried to make things in the virtual world as close to the same dimensions as objects in the real world, and often spent hours researching just the size and shape of inanimate objects. He also took copious notes on the way that things felt and smelled and, sometimes, tasted.

He'd already spent several hours working with Cody, and the boy had shown him the mechanics of how numerous things on the ranch worked, even the easy stuff like saddles and bridles. The kid was smart and quickly picked up on the simple physics Adam explained, then directed him to the kind of things that would help with the game's setting.

Adam had a surprisingly good time hanging out with the boy. He was clever and funny, and they got along well.

A noise from the barn drew his attention, and he looked up to see Skye and Clint run out of the barn and toward the stables. Cal and Cody followed at their heels.

"What's going on?" he asked Skye as she rushed past him.

"Fence is down. Cattle are getting out," she said, slowing down just long enough to tell him.

"Can I help?"

She hesitated a moment, then waved him on. "Sure, we could always use another hand."

Adam shoved the notebook and tape measure into his pocket and hurried after her. The group ran into the stable, but instead of getting horses, they headed for the group of four-wheeled quads that lined one wall.

He stopped, not knowing quite what to do as the four of them hopped onto the four available quads.

"You can ride with me, Skye," Clint offered. "That is, if Gamer Guy can handle a quad on his own."

Heat burned his cheeks. He had no idea how to ride one of the four-wheelers. He was sure he could figure it out, if he had some time, but it seemed as if time were of the essence.

"He hasn't signed a waiver, so he can just ride with me," Skye said, gesturing for him to climb on behind her, saving him from having to admit he had no clue how to drive one of these things.

"Sure, yeah, of course," Clint muttered, clearly not happy but not arguing against the liability issue.

Adam swung his leg over the seat, trying to leave a little room between him and Skye, just enough to be polite. But she pushed back against him, sending heat flooding through his veins as her rounded backside fit snugly against his thighs. "Hold on," she told him as she put the quad in gear and gunned the engine. The four of them tore out of the stable.

They didn't say anything as they rode. Adam was just trying to hold on as Skye maneuvered the quad over the rocky terrain of the hillside then through the pasture.

She raised a hand pointing to an area of downed fence line.

Forty to fifty cows were milling around the far pasture, and a lone cowboy was working to round up the farthest ones.

They all slowed as they approached the open area of fence, and Skye parked next to a fence post, then jumped off the quad. She yelled instructions to the others, circling her hands and pointing to where she wanted them to go. "We'll stay here and fix the fence. You all go round 'em up and get those cows back here."

Adam climbed off the quad, standing at the ready to help. "Just tell me what to do."

She opened the tool box affixed to the back of the quad and pulled out a small roll of wire and a couple sets of gloves. She tossed a pair to Adam. "Put these on. We're going to be working with barbed wire, and it can rip up your hands. But we need to get that fence repaired as fast as possible so we can close it up once they get all the cattle back through."

He nodded, pulling on the gloves as he walked toward the fence.

She worked quickly and efficiently, pulling out the length of fencing and looking for weak spots. "Check to see where the barbed wire is split or broken," she told him. Her focus was intent on her task. "We've got to recover the herd. Don't think of them as cattle that have gotten out; think of them as giant mooing bags of money that I'm liable to lose if we don't get them all rounded back up."

He nodded, understanding the seriousness of the job, and followed her lead, running his hands along the wire, looking for weak spots.

It didn't take them more than fifteen minutes of working together to get the fence repaired and ready.

The other men had been herding the cattle back through the gap, and they'd gotten all but the last few.

Adam held up a section of broken fence. The portion that was down had been part of a makeshift gate. But the wood appeared to be splintered, and the barbed wire had a clean, flat edge, almost as if it had been cut.

What the hell?

Chapter Seven

"Hey, Skye, you want to take a look at this?" Adam held up the suspicious section of wire. "Is there a chance someone let these cattle out on purpose?"

Skye raised an eyebrow at him. "Why would anyone do that? We had a massive windstorm the other night, and I'm sure that's what took this section out. I think you read too many mystery novels." She shook her head and bent back over the fence, twisting a piece of wire tightly around and not even bothering to look at the section he was holding out to her.

He shrugged and went back to work. She knew this kind of stuff better than he did.

"That's the last one," Cody yelled to his mom as he herded a brown-and-white cow through the gap.

The cow didn't seem to be in any hurry as it moseyed past Adam, who took a step back.

Cows were definitely bigger than they looked on television.

Skye waved the other men in, then lifted the repaired

section of fence and dragged it closed. She finished wiring the fence shut, pulled off her gloves, and tossed the tools back into the tool box.

Signaling toward the ranch, she straddled the quad, and Adam climbed back on and settled in behind her. Apparently they were all familiar with this kind of task and didn't need to do much talking. That and it was hard to hear over the roar of the four-wheelers' engines.

The ride back to the ranch wasn't as urgent, but Skye still drove quickly, and there were enough turns that Adam found himself hanging on to her waist.

Now that the crisis was over, he had time to savor the ride, enjoying both the view of the mountain landscape and the feel of the cowgirl spooned against him.

The ride ended much too quickly.

They parked the quads back in the stable. Skye turned off the engine and yelled her thanks to the rest of the crew, asking Cody to make sure the four-wheelers were gassed up again.

She smiled at Adam as they climbed off the quad. "You did good out there. I appreciate your help."

"I don't know how much I really helped, but I was glad to do it." He really had been glad. Besides getting to see and experience another side of ranch life, he got to spend time with Skye, and getting to wrap his arms around her again was an added bonus.

He liked seeing her in this environment, and surprisingly, he wasn't ready to go back to his room yet. "Do you need me to come with you and sign that waiver, since I was riding on the four-wheeler? I don't want to get anyone in trouble."

She leaned her head close to his ear, and the scent of her shampoo swirled in the air as she spoke softly. "You already signed all of the waivers we need when you registered for the camp. I just had a feeling you might not know how to drive one of the quads, and I didn't want you to be embarrassed."

"You felt right." Wait, that hadn't come out like he'd intended. Although it was true. "Er, I mean, your feeling about me not knowing how to operate one was correct." He shook his head. "You know what I mean."

She chuckled. "Yeah, I know."

He started to say something else, but Clint interrupted, calling to Skye from across the stable. "Hey, Skye, can you give me a hand with this?"

"I'd better go," she said, offering him an apologetic smile. "But maybe I'll see you at dinner?"

"Yeah, sure," he muttered and waved, but she'd already turned and headed toward Clint.

• • •

Adam let out a groan as he sank onto the bed in his room.

He'd just come back from that evening's meal, and he was in carb, and people, overload. The food had been a delicious feast of smoked meats, baked potatoes, and biscuits that had melted in his mouth, and the conversation had been fun, too. Skye had once again sat at their table and had finally drawn the dismal newlywed out of her shell.

And once again, Adam had mostly listened and tried not to watch Skye's mouth as she talked.

He'd actually had a good time talking to Josh about computers and gaming. The guy was smart, and he imagined, despite the fact that they were currently living in his parents' basement, he'd have a good chance of landing a pretty decent job.

But after spending the day making small talk and getting dirty—two things he abhorred—he was ready to be back in his room and away from people.

He might have stuck it out longer, but once he heard that Skye wouldn't be there, he'd lost interest in the evening's wagon ride.

Yesterday his feet had hurt—today everything hurt. He'd used muscles he didn't even know he had.

And now his body was achy and tired, but his mind was still going, his thoughts once again saturated with images of the blond cowgirl.

He took a shower, washing the dust of the ranch off his skin, and changed into shorts and a plain blue T-shirt. Picking up his book, he tried to settle into the story but found he couldn't focus.

It had been two days now that he hadn't had internet service. Apparently it was only available in certain areas of the lodge, and that was spotty at best. The frustration of finding a good spot to hold the signal hadn't been worth the effort, but he couldn't remember the last time he'd been away from cyberspace for so long. He could probably live for weeks without social media, but he felt disconnected from the world and his office without being able to check email and text messages.

He checked his cell phone. Still no service.

He tried with his laptop. No luck there, either.

Skye had said she had internet in her apartment. Maybe she'd let him connect for just a few minutes. Enough time to check his email and touch base with Ryan and Brandon.

She might have changed her mind and gone to the wagon ride with everyone else, but it wouldn't hurt to check. Right?

He stuffed his feet into the old pair of Converse he'd crammed into his bag at the last minute and picked up his laptop.

The worst that could happen was that she wouldn't be there.

Besides, hadn't he just spent the last two hours convincing himself that she would never be interested in a guy like him?

Best to just stop things now, stay in his room, get through

this week, figure out what he needed to do for the game, and go back to California and forget all about the cute cowgirl.

Two minutes later, he was knocking on her door.

His heart was actually hammering in his chest at the hope that she was there.

What was it about this woman that was turning him into an awkward teenage boy again? He thought he was over those days. He'd grown up. He was an intelligent, successful businessman that had his own company and a healthy stock portfolio. He had completed more than one master's degree, for frick's sake.

He spent plenty of time around beautiful women and didn't get flustered the way he did within thirty seconds of being in Skye's company.

This was ridiculous. She was just a woman. A woman with long blond hair and deep brown eyes—and luscious curves that could make a grown man weep.

Forget this. He needed to go back to his room—focus on something else. He didn't need the internet to work. He could go old school—use a pencil and paper and do some sketches and jot down some of his ideas for the new game.

He turned to go, resolute in his decision, but then he heard the door open. He glanced back, and his breath caught in his throat.

Skye was standing there, wearing a snug white tank top and a pair of cut-off shorts, her hair pulled back in a ponytail and her feet bare. Her legs were tanned and impossibly long, and her toes were painted a shimmery shade of pink.

She looked like an angel.

"Adam?"

He realized he was staring at her legs, entranced by the shapeliness of her calves, and he shook his head as if to clear his muddled brain. He offered her a sheepish grin. "Sorry, I'm not used to seeing you in shorts. You look amazing. Er…I mean, you look nice. Well, more than nice…I mean…" He clamped his lips together.

The grin on Skye's face widened. "Thanks. I think. Is there something I can do for you?"

Heat sprang to his neck as her question brought to mind several ideas, but somehow he doubted she meant those kinds of things. "Um…yeah. I was just wondering if…you said you had internet service in your apartment… I was hoping I might be able to plug in. Just to check my email and take care of a few things." Geez.

It had to be the shorts that were throwing him. Or the tank top and the way it hugged her breasts, the fabric just thin enough to show the outline of the lacy white bra she wore beneath it.

"Sure. Come on in." She held the door open, and he stepped into the room.

The apartment was surprisingly spacious with a large open living space on one side and a small kitchen on the other. A huge butcher block island separated the two spaces. An office and a bathroom were visible off the living room, and a short hallway led to what he assumed were bedrooms.

Skye's bedroom. He swallowed.

"My office is in here." She led him across the room and through a set of French doors, into a spacious study. Book shelves filled one wall, and a large desk filled the other. Stacks of books, some double-stacked, were crammed into one of the shelves, taking up every available space.

The other shelves were neatly organized with files and bins precisely labeled with information to run the ranch. He liked that she was both orderly with her business and cluttered with her leisure. Although his hands itched to reorganize her reading material into at least alphabetical order, if not by genre.

"This is really nice," he said, then his eye caught sight of her home computer. "Holy shit. Is that your PC?"

She frowned. "That's my computer, yes. Why? What's wrong with it?"

"Nothing was wrong with it, at least not when it came out. This thing is a dinosaur. And look how huge the hard drive is. How do you accomplish anything on this beast? Do you even have wifi, or is this still connected to dial-up?"

She planted her hands on her hips and cocked an eyebrow at him. "Do you want to use the internet or not?"

"Yes. Sorry. I do."

"Then I would suggest you quit making fun of Bess."

"Bess?"

She patted the top of the ancient computer. "That's what I call her. This old gal and I have been through a lot together."

"Like the eighties?" He held up his hands at the glare she gave him. "Okay, sorry. Nice to meet you, Bess. I've got a sassy spitfire for a grandmother, so I am partial to little old ladies. I'll be kind now."

"That's better." She pulled out the desk chair, and he sat down and pulled out his laptop.

"I'll just plug in to your Ethernet cord," he said, pushing her keyboard back to make room for his computer.

A stack of envelopes slid from underneath the keyboard, spilling across the desk and onto the floor. "Shit. I'm sorry." He reached for the envelopes, noting that several were stamped with red "Past Due" notices.

Skye scrambled to collect the envelopes, pulling open the desk drawer and shoving them inside. "Don't worry about it. I should have cleaned this up earlier."

He could tell by the way her cheeks tinged with pink and the flustered tone of her voice that she was obviously embarrassed that he'd seen them.

Cody was right. It seemed the place was in a bit of financial trouble. Or if all of those bills were past due, more than just a bit. No wonder she was so concerned about the cows getting out this afternoon.

Reaching under the desk, he found the Ethernet cable and feigned concentration on getting it connected to his laptop. "I really appreciate you letting me use your internet. I'm going crazy not being able to check my email. I didn't realize how connected to my gadgets I was until I couldn't use them for a few days."

"Yeah, it's amazing how addicted we get to our technology. But it's also kind of freeing just to turn them off and enjoy life."

"Yeah, but my idea of enjoying life is having eight solid, interruption-free hours to focus on work. Or maybe four hours to do nothing except immerse myself in a video game. Or a whole weekend to organize my office."

She raised her eyebrows. "Those are your best ways to enjoy life? What about getting outside, spending some time in nature?"

"In my book, nature is overrated."

"What? You live in one of the most beautiful states in the country. You have mountains *and* beaches. Do you live anywhere near the ocean?"

He nodded. "I'm actually just a few blocks from the beach. I can see the ocean from my living room window."

She sighed. "That sounds wonderful. Surely, you must take a lot of walks on the beach, or spend some time swimming in the ocean."

"Surely not. I'm not a fan of sand in my shorts, or between my toes, or in any of the other cracks and crevices that sand seems to find when you spend time on the beach. I do enjoy opening the window and listening to the ocean, though. If that counts for anything."

"It sounds to me like you are missing out. Didn't you spend a lot of time outside when you were a kid? Did your family ever go on vacation to national parks?"

"No. My mom was usually at work, so I was left to take care of my little brother. We were latchkey kids and Mom worried about us, so we went straight home after school and stayed inside until she got home from work."

"Gosh, I think I spent more time outdoors as a kid than I did inside. We went out as soon as we finished breakfast and only came back in to eat and sleep. I love the outdoors."

He shrugged. "I love working."

"Sorry. You said you needed to check your email, and here I'm keeping you. I'll let you get to it."

Crap. That's not what he'd meant. He loved talking to her. He could spend all night listening to her voice, to the slight country cadence she had when she spoke. "I wasn't hinting for you to leave."

She smiled, offering him a way out of his embarrassment. "It's okay. I've got some stuff to do anyway."

"Is that why you aren't on the wagon ride? I wasn't sure if you'd even be here. I figured you'd be down rolling along the trail, drinking cocoa, sitting on hay bales, and having straw poke you in the ass."

Seriously? Now he was thinking about her ass.

"You do know that's one of our most requested excursions. Most people love going on a hayride. They pay good money to spill hot cocoa on themselves and for that straw to poke them in the butt. And also to take a ride under the stars and to sing along to old country songs with the wagon master."

With Captain Cowboy.

Her voice held a dreamy tone as she described the scene, but it all sounded like a nightmare to him—the bugs, the dust, the forced proximity to a bunch of strangers whose shoulders and thighs would inevitably end up pressed against his. *No thank you.*

He probably shouldn't express those feeling to her. It

didn't sound like she shared his viewpoint on the experience.

"So why aren't you out there joining in on the sing-along fun?"

"I felt like I needed a little space tonight. And I think Cody did, too. I don't know if you noticed, but he seems a little interested in one of our guests. What's her name? Hannah? Katy? Something?"

"Haylee, I think."

"That's right. Wait, how did you remember that?"

"Cody may have mentioned something about her. But you didn't hear that from me. You know, Guy Code and all that."

She nodded. "That's what I thought. So I figured I'd let Cody have some time on his own tonight, and I would get a little time alone, too. I'm trying to let go a little, you know, give him more space and trust him more."

"Sounds smart. How you holding up with that idea?"

She blew out her breath. "I'm okay. I know he's getting older, and I have to let him have some freedom. It's just hard to let go. So, in order to distract myself from thinking about the fact that my son is growing up, I've made big plans for tonight involving a chick flick and some homemade chocolate chip cookies."

"Sorry that I messed that up."

"You didn't mess anything up." She gave him a shy smile. "I'm glad you're here. You're a good distraction, too. And you're welcome to join me for the movie and cookies."

Join her for a chick flick? He liked chick flicks about as much as he liked getting poked in the eye with a stick. "Yeah, sure. That sounds fun."

A smile tugged at the corner of her lips, and he loved it. He would sit through any number of romantic comedy viewing hours to earn that grin.

An insistent beeping sounded from the next room.

"That's the timer for the cookies. You want one?"

"Yes, please." He wanted one of everything she had to offer.

"Okay. I'll let you work and bring you some in a bit."

"Sounds good." Although the idea of him getting any work done at all with the scent of her skin lingering in the air and the sound of her puttering in the kitchen was pretty laughable. He couldn't concentrate on anything but her.

Opening his laptop, he pulled up his email and quickly scanned through the list of recent messages. Everyone at the company knew that he, Brandon, and Ryan were scheduled to be out this week, so his inbox was moderately small.

He did have a couple of messages from the guys filling him in on the troubles in London. Apparently the new release had surpassed their expectations, and the sheer volume of gamers downloading it had indeed crashed the server. They assured him they were working on a fix and were still hoping to join him later in the week.

He shot off a quick response filling them in on the last few days and giving them a quick summary of Cody's thoughts on the game.

Looking around at the outdated equipment, he also sent a quick email to his assistant, hitting send before he could change his mind. Then he closed his laptop and wandered back into the living room.

Skye was standing at the sink, washing the cookie sheets, and he could hear her softly singing as her foot tapped along to the tune obviously running through her head.

He was mesmerized by the soft bounce of her hips and couldn't tear his eyes from the place where the faded fringe of her shorts barely concealed the bottom of her butt.

She turned and caught him staring. Of course.

He held up a hand, offering her a small wave. "Hi."

Wow. His brilliant conversational skills at work again.

"Hi. You ready for a cookie?"

He nodded, his mouth watering at the smell of vanilla and chocolate in the air.

She motioned to the living room. "Have a seat. I'll bring some over. You want milk to go with them?"

"Sure."

Okay. This was different. Most of the women he dated were into fine wine and expensive entrees at fancy restaurants. He couldn't remember the last time he'd shared milk and cookies with someone.

He actually loved the idea.

Sinking onto the sofa, he spied Cody's gaming system, and an idea formed in his head.

Skye set a plate of cookies and two glasses of milk on the coffee table.

"So, I just had a thought," he said, then picked up a warm cookie and took a bite. The flavors of chocolate, butter, and sugar melted on his tongue, and he closed his eyes to savor the taste. "Holy shit. This is delicious. This just might be one of the best cookies I've ever tasted."

It was certainly made by the most beautiful woman he'd ever seen. That may have been coloring his evaluation, but he didn't think so. That cookie was just damn good.

"Oh stop it, you flatterer." She pushed against his leg, and his skin tingled where her fingers had touched.

"No, really. These are amazing." He reached for another then took a swig of milk. The combination seemed to warm him from the inside out, and he settled back against the cushions, aware of how close he sat to her and trying to calm his racing heart.

"You said you had an idea?"

"Oh yeah, right." He had the worst time concentrating when she was near. He couldn't seem to focus on anything except the smell of her hair and the nearness of her skin as her leg came close to brushing his. *Focus on the cookie. And the idea.*

He pointed to Cody's gaming system. "I was thinking about what you said. About how you feel like you have a hard time connecting with Cody. I was thinking I could teach you how to play *Masters of Misfortune* so you could play it with him. It might give you something in common to talk about."

Her eyes lit with excitement. "That sounds awesome."

"Yeah?"

"Yeah."

"Are you sure? Because before, you were saying that you didn't have time to play silly games like these. It was just an idea. You don't have to."

"It's a great idea. And I love that you were thinking of a way to help me connect with my son. It wouldn't be a waste of time if it actually works." She picked up the two game controllers that were in a basket on the coffee table and handed one to him. "How do we start?"

He turned on the equipment and had a tinge of pride that one of the *Misfortune* versions was already cued up. Maneuvering to a new game, he showed Skye how to choose her character (she picked Gemma, of course) and how to select an outfit and supplies for her.

Guiding her through the opening sequences, he showed her how to use the controller to move her character through the game. It didn't take long for Skye to catch on.

"Wow. This is really cool. I had no idea that this was what this game would be like. The graphics, or whatever you called them, look so realistic. I feel like I am really in the jungle. This is fun."

He loved watching her play the game he helped to create. Loved watching the delight cross her face as she discovered a new aspect of the mystery.

"I'm glad you like it," he said. "It makes me happy."

"Like it? I love it." She twisted her whole body as her thumbs worked the control, as if she could control the movements of the character by moving herself.

He loved it, too. Especially because every time she moved to the right, she brushed against him. And every time her bare leg touched his, it sent a sizzle of heat racing up his spine. And yeah, he probably could have just explained how to work the controller, but he liked resting his hand on top of hers as he guided her fingers.

Every time he touched her, his pulse quickened.

He seemed to be hyper-aware of all his senses—seeing her expressions, touching her hand, hearing the sound of her laughter, smelling the scent of her skin. The only one missing was taste, and he swallowed at the thought of sampling her lips, of nibbling her slender neck, of licking her…hell, her anything.

Sitting next to her was driving him mad, and he couldn't remember the last time he had wanted a woman so much.

It was killing him being so close, and sharing intimate space, yet not knowing if she was flirting or if he was reading her signals wrong. Maybe she was just a touchy person. He knew plenty of women like that, ones who were always touching your arm or something. They didn't mean anything by it, it was just their way.

Was that what was happening with Skye? Was she just a naturally affectionate person?

He didn't think so. He felt like they'd had an instant attraction—a spark. At least he had. Although for him, it was more than a spark… It was more like an explosion, an eruption of feelings that burst through his chest and ran hot through his veins.

Sitting next to her now, he felt like his skin was on fire, and his hands burned to touch her.

She was so animated when she played, her body bumping

against his as she moved around—her legs, her shoulder, her hand touching his as she pointed to a spot on the controller.

"This ledge is crazy. I've died ten times trying to make this jump. I can't make it across the river," she said, passing him her controller. "Can you just get me past this part so I can move on?"

Normally he wouldn't even consider it. It would take away from the game play and the integrity of the puzzle. But nothing about this was normal. And he was quickly realizing that he would do just about anything for Skye Hawkins—wear cowboy boots, muck out disgusting horse stalls, even attempt to country dance. Whatever she wanted.

He took the controller and easily maneuvered her character over the ledge and into the river.

"Oh no, be careful." She tapped his leg anxiously. "This is the part where my character usually drowns."

"I got this," he assured her with a laugh. But her enthusiasm was so contagious he played up the drama for her benefit. "I don't remember this being so tough, though. I might not make it after all."

But he knew he would. He'd designed this part and replayed every feature of it a hundred times. But he couldn't resist the way she clutched his arm and hopped up and down in her seat with anxiousness.

"Watch out for the crocodile," she shouted, pointing at the screen. "You're almost there."

He worked to manipulate the character so it swam past the crocodile and crawled out on the other bank, almost losing his concentration when she buried her head against his shoulder, laughing as she claimed she couldn't watch.

When she saw that he'd made it across the river to the other side, she let out a sigh of relief. "You did it." She gave him a hug. "Thank you for sharing this with me."

Adam caught his breath as her cheek pressed to his.

As if it had a mind of its own, his hand slid around her waist, pulling her to him as he hugged her back.

She drew back, but just slightly—just enough for him to see her face and take in her wide-eyed look of surprise.

His gaze dipped to her mouth—to her slightly parted rose-colored lips—and she inhaled a quick sharp pull of breath.

Not him. He couldn't breathe at all, couldn't move.

He was frozen in place, even though every synapse in his body was firing on all cylinders sending sparks of heat surging through his veins.

He looked back up, into her eyes, searching for a sign, anything that would tell him she was feeling the same thing, the same swirling sense of dizziness that had his own stomach in knots and his mouth going dry. Anything that would give him a glimpse of permission.

But she seemed to be frozen as well, suspended in the moment, as if she were waiting, afraid to move.

He leaned in—just a fraction of an inch—but close enough that his mouth was a whisper away from hers. She didn't pull back, and he moved the smallest bit closer and brushed her lips softly with his.

She sucked in a soft gasp, the tiniest sound but full of gigantic meaning. A sound that was a cross between pleasure and pain. It pierced his heart.

He stopped, not pressing, but not pulling away, as he felt the slight tremble of her lips against his. He waited, his heart pounding hard against his chest, somehow knowing that this moment could change everything.

Chapter Eight

Adam raised his free hand and set it gently against her cheek, cupping the side of her face, and she let out a soft moan—and it was about the sexiest thing he'd ever heard.

Heat streamed through his body, and he tilted his head just the slightest, and pressed his lips to hers.

A soft kiss, but full of meaning. Of promise.

Then another. Like a slow sip of an expensive glass of wine, he sampled her lips, testing her reaction.

Her lips parted, offering him an invitation, and he deepened the next kiss, slanting his mouth across hers and dipping his tongue between them.

She tasted like chocolate and cherry lip balm and what he was pretty sure heaven would be like.

The rest of the world fell away. Nothing mattered except this moment, this second in time.

Blood rushed to his ears as she pressed back, meeting his kiss with a sudden urgency as her fingers tightened against his back, then gripped handfuls of his T-shirt.

He slid his hand down her cheek, across her neck and

shoulder then clasped her arm, pulling her tightly to him.

She pressed closer, her soft curves melting against him, and he had to remind himself to breathe.

He pulled back, his breath ragged and shaky, already missing the soft feel of her lips.

Aw hell, breathing is overrated anyway.

He leaned back in, capturing her mouth in another kiss, this one filled with heat and passion and a crazy sense of desperation that he had no idea where it was coming from.

But he did know he wanted her. *Needed* her. Knew that his skin felt like it was on fire, and having her was the only way to extinguish the flames.

He drew his hand down her arm, skimming the side of her breast, and she let out another low moan against his lips.

Pressing her back against the sofa, he kissed the corner of her mouth, then her jaw, then laid a line of kisses along her neck and across her chest. Her tank top had shifted, revealing her creamy breasts as they pushed out of the top of her lacy bra, and he ran his tongue along her pale skin at the edge of the white lace.

She squirmed under him, arching her back and dropping her head back against the sofa.

His hand slid up her ribs to cup her breast, feeling the hardened pebble of her nipple through the fabric of her bra as he skimmed his thumb across it, eliciting another soft gasp.

She let out a gasp of need, of desperate desire, and something broke inside of him. A defensive wall that he'd built around his heart crumbled and fell as her body trembled beneath him.

Hunger spiraled inside of him, stirring in every cell of his body, as he tugged the top of her bra down, then filled his palm with her exposed breast, pushing it up as he circled her taut pink nipple with his tongue.

Her fingers dug into his back, urgent and insistent as he

drew the hardened tip between his lips, sucking the bud as he kneaded her breast.

Her body was perfect, and he ached to see—and touch—more of it. *All* of it.

Sliding his hand down her waist and hips, he cupped the impeccable curve of her butt, skimming his fingers along the bare skin at the frayed edge of her shorts.

A low growl sounded in his own throat, a hum of need and hunger, as he feasted on her skin, kissing each breast then her chest, her neck, the line of her jaw.

He pulled the ponytail holder from her hair, letting it fall across her shoulders, and he drove his hands through it, clutching the silky strands as he buried his face in her neck.

Pulling her body against his, he shifted them so he could lay her back against the sofa, then he pulled back, filling his gaze with the vision of her. Her hair was tousled and spread across the couch, and her shirt was disheveled, pulled down on the side, so that one bare breast spilled over the top.

She looked gorgeous, sexy as hell, like a fantasy. Except this was real. This was actually happening.

He leaned down and slanted his mouth over hers, crushing her lips in an onslaught of desire.

Her leg circled his, pulling him tighter to her, as she yanked up the back of his T-shirt.

Everything else fell away. All of his focus was on her. Touching her. Kissing her. Feeling her.

He couldn't get enough.

Nothing else mattered.

Nothing except the subtle whisper of clicks that sounded as someone inserted a key into the lock of the front door.

Adam sprang back, and panic filled Skye's eyes.

"It's Cody." She struggled to sit up, hastily adjusting her top and smoothing down her hair.

Adam shifted in his seat, grabbing a throw pillow and

holding it in his lap, fervently trying to think of baseball stats or something that might diminish his raging erection. Thank goodness he wore loose shorts.

The game controllers were scattered on the floor, and he reached for one, quickly hitting a key that started the game playing again, while he struggled to catch his breath.

He felt like he'd had the wind knocked out of him, as if a tornado had just swirled through the room, lifting them up and tossing them around in a passion-filled storm.

He sucked in a deep breath as the door swung open and Cody walked in.

The boy stopped in his tracks, glancing from them sitting on the sofa to the television, and his forehead creased in annoyance. "Hey, what do you guys think you're doing?"

"Cody, listen, it was my fault," Adam answered, searching his brain for a way to explain. But his mind refused to work; his thoughts were still muddled with images of Skye. It was as if he could still feel her against him.

But somehow he didn't think Cody would be thrilled with any explanation of why he'd been mauling his mother on the living room couch.

He snuck a glance at Skye. Her mouth was open, as if she wanted to say something but no words would come out. All Adam could think about was the way her lips had that just-kissed swell to them, which did not help his attempts to quell his own problem. He readjusted the pillow.

But Cody's eyes were fixed on the television screen. "Are you guys playing my game? Did you mess up my level?"

Adam let out a relieved sigh.

"Don't worry. Yours is safe. We started a new game."

"Why?"

"Because I wanted to learn how to play it," Skye said, finally managing to speak.

"You did?"

"Yeah, I did. You're always wanting to talk about it, so Adam offered to teach me how the game works. Maybe we could even play it together."

Cody's eyes narrowed with skepticism as he glanced between her and Adam. Then his face broke into a grin. "Really? You actually learned how to play *Masters of Misfortune*? For me?"

Her face lit up, and something inside of Adam lit as well—like a little pang of happiness at his role in coming up with the idea.

"Of course for you. I'm not very good at it. But I'm trying."

Cody dropped onto the sofa next to her and reached for a controller. "You must be pretty good if you got past the river. It took me forever to figure that part out. I kept getting eaten by the crocodile."

She laughed, and the sound was music to his ears. "Me, too. I couldn't even get to the crocodile. I kept getting swept into the rapids and drowning. Adam helped me with that part."

"What?" Cody cocked an eyebrow at him. "Dude."

Adam held up his hands in surrender. "I know. I should have let her do it herself. But I couldn't help it."

The boy shook his head. "I probably would have helped her, too. That part is totally ridiculous. I wish I knew the guy that created the game so I could tell him what I think."

Adam chuckled. "I'm all ears."

Cody looked at his mom. "So do you still want to play? Like a game with me?"

Adam felt Skye stiffen next to him, and then she reached between them and clasped the side of his shorts, gripping a fistful of the fabric.

"Yeah. Sure. I'd like that."

Cody fiddled with the controller to maneuver the screen to a fresh game, then leaned around his mom to look at Adam.

"I have an extra controller if you want to play with us. But I get to be Vic."

Adam laughed again. He liked this kid. "You're on. I like playing Theo better anyway. I've got to warn you, though, I do have a bit of an advantage. But I'll try to let you guys do the majority of the tasks."

"I'll warn you," Cody said. "I'm pretty good, too."

He clamored from the sofa to dig the extra controller out of a basket of game paraphernalia that sat on the shelf under the television.

Skye snuck an excited glance at him, and he gave her hand a squeeze.

"Here ya go." Cody passed him a controller. "It's the original one that came with the setup, so the grips are worn and the X button sometimes sticks. That can be your disadvantage."

Adam let go of Skye's hand before Cody saw it and took the game device.

They settled in to play, and Adam was surprisingly happy to let Cody take the lead in explaining the game to his mom. It was fun for him to hear how the boy explained challenges and what his take was on the puzzles, plus he got a kick out of listening to them both laugh as they traversed through the jungles of Peru, united in their quest to find the treasure.

They had plenty of gamers that tested their products and helped them find bugs in their games, but this was different. This was just ordinary people enjoying something he'd helped to create.

His chest swelled with a mixture of pride and happiness that his game was also helping to bring this mom and son together—to give them a common interest. He never imagined people like Skye being part of the target audience, but the wheels in his head were already spinning about how they could create some type of family-play version in the next game.

Just by listening, Adam was picking up a lot of ideas about what to include in their new product.

"Watch out for that snake," Skye shouted, pointing to the screen.

"I see it. Calm down, Mom," Cody admonished, then laughed. "You just take care of collecting the artifacts. I'll take care of the jungle creatures."

"You're so close. Just a few more steps." She bounced in her seat. "Adam, get that statue. We're almost to the top."

He gladly followed her instructions, and the three of them guided their characters up the stairs and into the ancient tomb. Racing through a series of tunnels, they came out into a large, cavernous room filled with treasures. Waterfalls rained from spouts in the sides of the walls, and golden sunlight spilled into the room, sparkling off the piles of gold.

"Wow," Cody whispered, his voice filled with awe as he stared at the screen. "This is so freaking cool."

"This is amazing," Skye agreed.

"Wouldn't it be so cool to actually be *in* this video game and have to scale the walls yourself, and then you get to walk into this room? That would be awesome."

"That would be cool." Skye nudged Adam. "Could you please work on that? We'd like an option to actually crawl inside your video game and be part of the action."

Adam laughed. "I'll get right on it." His mind was already racing with the possibilities.

• • •

Skye let out a yawn, then glanced up at the clock on the wall.

It was almost midnight.

How could that be?

They had spent the last two hours playing, wandering

around the treasure room and amassing artifacts to use in the next level. She'd been totally immersed in the game and in the fun she was having with both Cody and Adam, and she hadn't realized how late it was.

She stifled another yawn. "You guys, we've got to quit. We've got a big day tomorrow with the cattle drive and the camp-out. We need to get some sleep."

"Aw, come on, Mom. Ten more minutes?" Cody pleaded.

She couldn't remember the last time her son had begged to spend another ten minutes with her. "Okay, ten more minutes. Then that's it. No complaints. We're turning it off and going to bed."

Sneaking a glance at Adam, she caught him raising his eyebrows teasingly at her comment about going to bed.

A grin tugged at the corners of her lips, and she nudged him with her elbow. "Be good," she mouthed.

"I plan to be," he said quietly against her ear, before he reached forward and took the last cookie from the plate.

Heat bloomed in her chest at the thought of sleeping with Adam, at how "good" it could be. From the way he had kissed her earlier, she imagined it would range somewhere in the category between "amazing" and "spectacular," bordering on "mind-blowing."

His first kiss had been toe-curling enough, and her inner muscles clenched as she fantasized about what could have happened if Cody hadn't come home.

Would Adam have taken her to bed?

Would she have wanted him to?

This was crazy. And seemed to be happening way too fast. She couldn't believe how far and how fast that first kiss had gone, how quickly they'd both become carried away in the moment. He'd gone from touching her hand to first base in a matter of minutes.

And the craziest thing was…she'd wanted him to. Wanted

him to touch her, and reveled in the fact that they'd been so caught up in the heat of passion that he was pulling aside her clothes. The thought of his hand, and his mouth, on her breast had her skin heating even now.

The fact that things had happened so quickly told her there was something special about this guy. They had chemistry.

Still, her actions had surprised her. She hadn't kissed a man in years, and yet, she was suddenly considering jumping into bed with Adam.

Could she just be desperate to have a man's hands on her?

No, she knew she wasn't like that. Besides, she'd had plenty of opportunity to date, if she'd wanted to. But she hadn't.

There was only one man in her life. Well, one boy, that she was busting her butt to turn into a man. A fine man, who respected women, and who wouldn't leave.

Not like his father, who had left before he'd even met Cody. Skye had been nine months pregnant when she'd turned up on her father's doorstep with a suitcase, a swollen belly, a tear-stained face, and a promise to herself to never trust another man with her heart.

And she hadn't. It was easier to turn guys down, right at the start. She didn't need to date. She wasn't even sure she ever wanted another man in her life.

But then a tall, dark-haired computer whiz had stepped off the bus, wearing a frown and a pair of awful snakeskin cowboy boots, and her heart had stumbled in her chest.

Who would have thought that a guy who'd never even been on a horse would be the one to finally jumpstart her heart?

And her libido.

One touch of Adam's lips and she was right back in the old saddle again…er…so to speak. Her mind might have put those feelings aside, but her body remembered, responding to his touch with a fire and intensity that she didn't even know she had in her.

But evidently she did. And not just a little flame, but apparently a freaking inferno.

Just thinking about it had licks of heat darting up her spine, and she barely resisted squirming in her seat.

Focus on the game, girl.

They were only going to play for ten more minutes. So, she had ten more minutes of feeling Adam's thigh pressed against hers, of smelling his amazing aftershave, of having her bare arm brush against his bicep.

Thirty minutes later, they were still playing.

"We have to stop," she said, setting down her controller and finally calling it quits.

"Okay. Okay," Cody conceded, dropping his controller on the sofa and giving his mom a quick one-armed hug. "I'm going to bed. Thanks for playing, Mom. That was cool." He waved at Adam as he headed for his bedroom. "Good night, Adam. Thanks for teaching my mom to play *Misfortune*."

"Good night. See you tomorrow."

Skye sat perfectly still, unable to move, stunned at the actions of her son.

"You okay?" Adam asked, turning to her as the door of Cody's room thumped shut.

She shook her head slowly. "Did you see that? My son just gave me a hug. And thanked me for hanging out with him." She raised her head, her gaze meeting Adam's. "Thank you. Thank you for teaching me to play this game. For having this idea."

He shrugged. "It was no big deal."

"It *was* a big deal." She rested her hand lightly on his leg. "Everything about tonight was a big deal."

A shy smile crossed his face, and he glanced down at her hand. "Yeah. It was for me, too. I wish…" He stopped.

"You wish what?"

He shook his head. "Nothin'. It's late. I'd better let you get to bed." He set his controller next to hers and pushed up from the sofa. He stretched his arms above his head and let out a yawn. His shirt rose above his waistband, offering her a glimpse of the tight muscles of his abdomen, and she wanted to reach out and run her fingers across the band of skin.

"How do you stay in such great shape when you work in an office all day?" She stood up and followed him to the door.

He grabbed his computer on the way. "Brandon, one of my partners, is a big health nut. He had a workout room installed at our office and insists that we all work out together three or four times a week. We usually strategize as we lift and do cardio. It works out pretty well—keeps us in fighting shape." He laughed as he patted his stomach.

"They sound like great guys." She opened her front door and stepped into the empty hallway with him.

"They are. And we usually do whatever Brandon tells us to do. Except when he tried to get us to drink kale smoothies. We drew the line at that one."

"I hope I get to meet them."

"I'd hoped so, too. But from the last email they sent, it's not sounding likely. But don't worry. I'll still pay for their stay here."

"That's fine. Whatever you want to do," she said casually, although she was breathing an inner sigh of relief. She didn't want to tell Adam that she needed their registration fees to pay one of her overdue bills. It was embarrassing enough that he'd caught sight of those bills scattered on the floor of her office. Hopefully, he hadn't realized what they were.

"And I'll cover their fees for the excursions, too. I know the cattle drive and the camp-out was an extra fee, and I'll make sure that's covered, even though they didn't show up. In fact, maybe I'll throw in a bit extra, just to make up for the inconvenience."

Apparently he did realize it. "You don't have to do that."

"I want to. I want to help."

Even though his words were spoken in earnest, her back still bristled. Did he feel sorry for her? She already had Clint offering to swoop in to save her. Now Adam was going to try, too? Did she seem that desperate? "I don't need your charity."

He reared back slightly at the hostility of her tone. "It's not charity. It's business. Besides, it's not a big deal. I'd just like to help you out. Because I can."

Where was this coming from? Did he have some kind of white-knight complex? Did he think he was some rich guy coming in to help the poor country girl? Screw that. "Sorry, I'm not trying to be nasty about it, but I've come a long way to prove that I can run this ranch on my own. I can take care of myself. I don't need your help, or anyone's."

"Except for Captain Cowboy's," he muttered, his gaze going to a spot on the carpet.

"What did you say?"

He sighed and looked back up at her. "I said, except for that guy, Clint. You seem to be okay taking his help."

"Not that it's any of your business, but I don't *take* his help. We barter for services. He doesn't work on the ranch for free. He does it in exchange for *my* help."

"You're right. It isn't any of my business." He took a step back, hurt and embarrassment evident on his face. "I should probably just go."

"Yeah, you probably should." Annoyance and defeat swirled through her chest as she stepped back into her apartment and shut the door behind her.

Chapter Nine

Breakfast the next morning proved to be an ordeal, as Skye did her best to avoid looking at Adam, or crossing paths with Adam, or mentioning Adam's name, all while her traitorous eyes kept trying to sneak glances at him.

He must have visited the gift shop again, because he showed up at breakfast wearing one of the blue flannel shirts they sold. She didn't know whether to feel glad for the sale or insulted that he was trying to find another way to offer her charity.

The shirt did look good on him, though. So did the boots. Dang. Why did he have to look so freaking cute?

And why did she start to sweat every time she thought about that kiss?

Although calling it just a kiss didn't do it justice. It was more like a toe-curling, spine-tingling, heat-filled lip assault. And that was putting it mildly.

Looking at him this morning, with his glasses slightly askew and a shock of his dark hair still sticking up from where he'd just run his hand through it, he didn't appear to be the suave, charming guy that had knocked her socks—and her bra—off.

The rest of her breakfast companions had already left, but she still sat at her table, nibbling on the last of a butter-covered biscuit, while she tried not to look at him.

Adam was still at his table, too, apparently deep in conversation with Josh, the young newlywed.

Skye studied him for a moment, his expression intense as he nodded, apparently agreeing with whatever the other man was saying.

Looking at him now, there didn't appear to be anything special about the guy. Sure, he was cute, and he had a great body, slim and lean and muscled just enough so that you could see the outline of his bicep straining against the fabric of his shirt.

But she knew plenty of guys who were cute and muscular. What was the big deal about this one? Why did the thought of him keep her awake most of the night as she relived that make-out session on the sofa?

He is just a guy, she reminded herself. A guy that lived in California, who would be here for only a few more days. A guy who didn't have a place in her world and who would soon be walking out of her life. Just like every other guy.

Adam wasn't any different. He wasn't special.

Then he grinned at something Josh said, and her insides went loopy, and her heart suddenly felt too big for her chest.

She took a deep breath, fighting the sudden sting of tears in her eyes. *Where the hell did that come from?*

Swallowing back the sudden emotion, she turned away, busying herself with cleaning up the table and putting the condiments back in their place at the center. Staring into her lap, she twisted the corner of her napkin between her fingers.

She needed to forget about Adam Clark. She *knew* he was going to leave. He had to leave. He had a life somewhere else.

No—it was best to just forget about him altogether. Focus on her work, the ranch, her son.

"Is this seat taken?"

Her head jerked up as Adam pulled out the chair next to her and sat down.

The scent of his now familiar aftershave mingled with the smell of maple syrup filled the air around her, and her pulse quickened.

"Um…no…I mean, hi," she stammered. He didn't touch her, but she swore she could feel the heat of his skin as his leg rested less than an inch from hers.

"Listen, Skye, I'm sorry about last night. I hated the way we left things."

She let out a shaky breath. "Me, too."

"I thought about what you said. Actually I thought about you all last night. I don't think I slept at all."

She blinked. He'd stayed up all night thinking about her?

He waited a beat, as if hoping she might return the sentiment, but she didn't know what to say.

"Anyway, I wanted to tell you that I'm sorry, and that last night really meant something to me. *You* mean something to me. I don't usually act like that."

She sighed. "It's just that I've been on my own for a long time. I don't need someone to come in and act like they know what's best for me."

He shook his head. "I wouldn't dream of suggesting that I know what's best for you. I was just trying to help. That's how my brain works. I see a problem, and I try to fix it."

"But I don't need anyone to fix me."

His hand rested on the table next to hers. He stretched out his thumb and gently stroked it across the edge of her hand, sending a shiver down her spine.

"I wasn't trying to fix *you*. You are perfect. Couldn't you tell? I acted like a sex-starved teenager, something I never do.

But you just make me kind of crazy."

Crazy? She tried to pull her hand back, but he reached out and grabbed it instead. His skin was warm as he squeezed her fingers against his palm.

"Crazy in a *good* way. Like in an 'I can't stop thinking about you—I'm crazy *about* you' kind of way." He leaned closer and lowered his voice. "And last night, when I kissed you, I did feel like a teenager. I don't know what came over me, but I couldn't think straight, couldn't think at all. And I definitely couldn't keep my hands off of you."

Heat warmed her chest, and her mouth went dry. He'd just said he was "crazy about her." She swallowed. This whole thing was crazy.

"Thanks, Skye. Breakfast was great," Josh called out as he and Brittany left the dining hall.

She pushed back in her chair, shaking her head, and dropped Adam's hand so she could wave at the newlyweds. It was as if she'd forgotten for a moment that they were still at the breakfast table, surrounded by guests. "We'll see you guys this afternoon."

Adam cleared his throat, looking around as if he, too, had just noticed they weren't alone.

He changed his tone to a more professional, less intimate one. "So anyway, like I was saying, I do see a problem with the efficiency of your office equipment. Even though Bess, your antiquated but familiar computer system, is great, she could use a serious upgrade. And that's something I can easily help with. I work for a company that deals with computers, and we have to keep up with the latest technology. We literally have dozens of computers that are only a few years old sitting in a storage room, waiting to be recycled or donated or used for spare parts. You would actually be helping me by taking a few off my hands."

"But..."

"Before you say anything, I want you to know that I heard what you said last night about Cowboy Clint and how you barter for services. So I came up with what I think is a suitable trade. I want to upgrade your technology for the lodge and make life easier for you. You want to upgrade my appreciation for nature and make life better for me. Right?"

"Right."

"So how about if we strike a deal? A barter, if you will. You let me install a little bit of technology to update your system, and I'll let you introduce me to the finer points of nature and try not to grumble too much about getting dirt on my clothes." He offered her a friendly grin.

He'd obviously thought this through. How could she say no? "Are they *really* old computers that you don't use anymore? I know computer equipment is expensive, and I wouldn't feel right letting you spend money on me like that."

He drew an X on his chest. "Cross my heart. We literally have a storeroom full of old equipment that will probably just get recycled anyway. If you were to take it, it would clear stuff out of our storage space, and it will make me feel better about our upgrades, knowing that someone is putting the old stuff to good use."

She grudgingly held out her hand. "Okay. You've got a deal."

He took her hand and held it in his for just a moment too long. "Good."

"But I'm not gonna take it easy on you with this nature stuff. Since we're already doing a camp-out tonight, I'm thinking we need to add a hike up the bluff and fire-making lessons."

"I'm all in."

"Prepare to get dirty."

A naughty grin spread across his face.

She laughed. "I didn't mean it like that." Not entirely. But now that she thought about it, maybe she did.

• • •

Adam shifted in the saddle and squeezed his legs around his horse's middle, trying desperately to hold on. He was fine when the beast was just walking, but it made him nervous every time it sped up, bouncing him around while it jogged or trotted or whatever Skye had called it.

A "sore ass" was what he called it. But he was trying to be a good sport. What was the worst that could happen anyway? The horse could buck him off, and he could break his arm in the fall, then get trampled by the hundreds of cows they were moving from one ridge to another and end up hospitalized or dead. Other than that, no big deal.

He might not have ever ridden a horse before, but he'd seen the old John Wayne movie *The Cowboys* and knew what happened when a guy fell off his horse into a stampede of cows. Especially when it was the kid with the glasses. It was always the kid with the glasses.

Good thing he was wearing his contacts today. At least he had that going for him.

His horse stopped and bent its head down to eat some grass. This wasn't really much of a stampede anyway. It was mostly a group of slow-moving cows that plodded along quite amiably, as if they somehow knew they were being moved to another pasture with better grass.

Hell, maybe they did know.

His horse took another bite of grass, dragging Adam's body forward as he struggled to stay in the saddle.

"How you doing, cowboy?" Skye asked, riding up next to him on the right.

He didn't even look up. All of his concentration was on wrestling with the reins and trying to pull his horse's head back up. "Just grand. Having the time of my life," he muttered.

She chuckled and kept riding forward, clucking to his horse to follow. "Ah, come on. It's not all bad. Have you checked out the view?"

He lifted his head in her direction as the horse took a step forward, and his breath caught in his throat. Not just at the amazing backdrop of the mountains, but of her.

Skye was a vision. She sat tall in her saddle, her back straight, the reins held loosely in her hands as she maintained complete control over her horse. A straw cowboy hat sat low across her forehead, and wisps of her long blond hair swirled in the air around her, carried by the light breeze. Or possibly fairies. Because in that moment, she looked magical.

But she was real. Her smile was real. And it was all for him.

As gorgeous as she was now, sitting on that horse with the mountain scenery behind her, she'd been just as beautiful when he'd kissed her the night before.

Images of feasting on her bare skin filled his mind, and heat surged through his veins. But that wasn't all that was surging. He shifted in the saddle, his jeans suddenly tighter.

Geez, he needed to get a grip before he fell off this damn horse.

"You're right," he called to her. "It is an amazing view."

She laughed, as if she knew exactly what he was thinking. "Hang in there. We're almost to the place where we'll split from the group. Clint and Cal will finish taking the cattle on to the pasture and our bunch will head up the ridge to the spot where we're going to set up camp for the night."

"I'm good. I could do this all day."

"Yeah, right. You're being a good sport anyway. It's really not too much farther. Just over the next hill." She left him with a wave and galloped ahead.

The group spent another twenty minutes riding up a small

hill and herding the cows forward. The terrain opened up to a wide expanse of pasture on one side and a rocky ridge on the other. Pine trees dotted the side of the hill, but he could see a trail heading up through the trees.

Skye spent a few minutes going over the final details with Clint.

Adam tried not to sneer every time he looked at the handsome cowboy. The guy was totally at ease on his horse. He had the confidence and look of the Marlboro man, and watching Skye laugh at something Clint said grated on Adam's nerves.

He turned to Josh, who had ridden up next to him. "How's it going? Are you enjoying your first cattle drive?"

The younger man's smile was contagious. "Heck, yeah. This is awesome." He jerked a thumb toward his bride, who was a few yards away, wearing her usual sullen expression. "Brittany is not enjoying it quite as much."

"I guess this kind of activity isn't for everyone."

Josh shrugged. "She's usually really fun. But every time something goes wrong on this trip, I know she's sorry we came. I keep telling her that someday we'll be able to take a beach vacation, but right now, we need to save our money until I find a job."

"Sounds sensible."

"Yeah, we don't want to be living in my parents' basement forever. She gets that, but stepping in a giant pile of horse poop this morning didn't improve her attitude about this place."

Adam chuckled then turned his attention to Skye, who'd called them toward her to offer them instructions on the next section of their ride.

He, Josh, and Brittany had signed up for a camp-out on the top of the ridge. Cody and Skye would be taking them on to the campsite, while the rest of the group headed back to the ranch to spend their nights in comfortable beds.

Each of their horses was packed with supplies for the camp-out to evenly distribute the weight. Adam's horse carried his tent, sleeping bag, and a saddlebag full of food.

Skye had his things stored in one of her saddlebags. She'd told him to pack light for the trip but had seemed surprised when he'd handed her the clean T-shirt and a Ziploc bag containing a stick of deodorant, a toothbrush with a small tube of toothpaste, and a fresh pair of boxer briefs.

He'd only shrugged. "You said pack light. This is pretty much all a guy needs for a two day trip."

She'd laughed and shoved them into one of the bags hanging off the side of her saddle.

"Let's go," Skye called, leading her group toward the hillside. The air cooled as they plodded into the shade of the trees, and it would have been much more pleasant if Adam hadn't been clinging to the saddle on a half-ton beast as they began the ascent up the side of the mountain.

The end of his tent bumped against his leg as his horse climbed along the rocky trail.

Skye had assured him that the horse knew what it was doing, that it didn't want to fall any more than he did, but it still made him nervous every time the horse's footing stumbled on the loose gravel.

His knuckles were white as he gripped the saddle horn, his stomach pitching each time the horse faltered.

They came through a set of trees and stopped in a clearing. Evidently he wasn't the only one whose nerves were on edge.

The young bride was apparently not enjoying herself, either. Her face was drained of color, and she had a death grip on her horse's mane as it plodded into the clearing. She let out a string of swear words as she threw her leg over the saddle and staggered to the ground.

"I'm done," she cried, her voice breaking as the tears

started. "I'm not getting back on that horse."

"What's wrong?" Josh asked, climbing off his horse and coming to his young bride's aid.

"I hate this. That stupid horse keeps turning its head back and trying to bite my leg, and I'm terrified I'm going to fall off. I just want to go back."

"But we already paid for the excursion," Josh explained, putting an arm around her shoulder.

"I don't care. I don't care about the money. I don't care about the adventure. I just want to go back to the lodge," she wailed. "If you're so worried about it, you can go on without me and spend the night in a stupid tent by yourself. But I'm going back, even if I have to walk."

Skye slipped off her horse and threw her reins over a low set of branches on a nearby tree. She crossed to Brittany, resting a hand on her shoulder as she spoke quietly. "It's okay. You don't have to go. This is supposed to be fun. We're not going to make you do something that makes you this upset. Why don't we take a break and have a little snack. You'll have a chance to rest a few minutes."

Brittany nodded and let Skye lead her over to a small outcropping of boulders. Skye got her settled on the rocks, then passed out granola bars and small boxes of raisins to the group. They each had been given a trademark "Hawkins Ridge Ranch" water bottle, and they ate the snacks and had some water as the rest of the group dismounted and stretched their legs.

But even after a twenty-minute break, Brittany wasn't to be dissuaded. She stuck to her guns, insisting that her horse had it in for her, and she wasn't getting back on it.

Skye assured her it was okay to go back, but it was a long walk to the ranch. She finally convinced her to get on Cody's horse with him. "He's a good rider. You'll be safe with him. And he can just lead your horse back to the ranch."

Cody's shoulders straightened at his mother's praise, and he helped pull Brittany onto the saddle behind him. He looked over at Adam, then back at his mom. "You guys going to be okay? I can drop these guys back at the ranch and come back up to the ridge."

Skye shook her head. "Don't worry about us. We'll be fine. I packed Adam's tent and sleeping bag on his horse, and we've got plenty of food for the two of us."

The boy's mouth was set in a thin line as he glanced back at Adam. Had he picked up on the mounting sexual tension between him and his mother? "But what if you get in trouble? How is he going to help you?"

Oh, nice. The kid wasn't concerned about anything romantic happening; he was just worried that Adam wasn't capable of taking care of his mom if something happened. Although, now that he thought about it, what the hell would he do if something happened?

Calm down. What was going to happen? They were just going camping, for frick's sake. Camping in the wilderness with snakes, and bears, and mountain lions. Shit. Maybe he should go back to the lodge. Brittany had given him an easy out.

He glanced at Skye. Her knowing grin seemed to suggest that she already figured he was going to bail.

Forget that. They'd made a deal, and he'd agreed to give her a chance to turn him on to nature. But who could pay attention to nature when she was around, turning him on already just standing there.

"We'll be fine," he assured Cody. It did rankle him to think that the boy probably wouldn't have given it a second thought if it were Cowboy Clint who was spending the night out on the ridge. Clint could take care of anything.

Cody gave his mother one last questioning glance, then seemed satisfied as she nodded and passed him the reins of

Brittany's horse.

"You can help Cal with the cookout tonight, then sleep over at his place. He'll be glad to have the extra hand."

Cody's face brightened a little, and Adam suspected that it had more to do with seeing Haylee at the cookout tonight than the opportunity to sleep on the older ranch hand's couch.

"See you in the morning, then." Cody turned, and the mare fell in step behind them as he led it and Josh back down the trail.

Skye sat down on the boulder next to Adam. "That just leaves us. Are you sure you're okay staying? It's all right if you want to go back."

"Heck no. I'm pumped."

She chuckled and raised an eyebrow at him. "Yeah?"

"Maybe not exactly *pumped*, but moderately enthusiastic," he answered with a shrug. "Besides, we made a deal. And I keep my promises."

Her laughter died. "That's not been my experience with the men in my life," she muttered as she stood and wiped the dust off her pants. "Let's head out, then. We want to have time to get the tents set up and have dinner made before the sun goes down. Once it dips behind the ridge, the temperature drops a good ten to fifteen degrees."

Skye was all business as she cleared up their trash, tightened their saddlebags, and then swung herself easily up onto her horse.

He was a little less graceful as he grabbed the saddle horn and hauled himself back into his horse's saddle.

They rode in silence for the next half hour, which was fine with Adam. He needed his full concentration to hold on as the horse climbed up the steep trail. Trying not to cringe every time the horse faltered on the gravel, his nerves were shot by the time they reached the top of the ridge and rode out of the clearing.

"What do you think?" Skye asked, stopping her horse so his could catch up and stand next to hers. "Pretty amazing, huh?"

He'd been so focused on staying upright in the saddle, he hadn't really paid much attention to his surroundings, except for the random pine branch that he either had to duck under or pull his leg back to avoid getting scraped by.

But he raised his head now, and his breath caught in his throat as he took in the majestic scenery around him. The clearing reminded him of a photograph he'd seen in a book, almost too beautiful to be real. Bright green expanses of grass were dotted with a colorful array of wildflowers. Another row of mountains lay beyond it, their snow-capped peaks blindingly white against the brilliant blue sky. A thin river ran through the center of the clearing, winding down from the mountains then disappearing into the dense forest.

His chest tightened, and he swallowed back the sudden emotion that filled his throat. He had no words to explain his response and wasn't sure he could speak, even if he did know what to say. All he could do was nod.

A smile broke across Skye's face. "I told you."

They sat in silence for a few minutes, just taking in the view, and then Skye pointed to a spot where the river narrowed in size. "We'll cross there. The river is shallow enough in that spot that the horses can walk across it. Then we'll camp over there, next to the bluff. That'll keep the wind away and still give us a great view."

"Sounds good." His horse fell in step behind hers and they traveled through the grassy area, walking along the bank of the river. The path there was still a little rocky, but not as steep, and Adam was just starting to relax when he heard a sound that made his blood run cold.

His horse let out a terrified whinny and reared up as the rattlesnake coiled in the path below them, poised to strike.

Chapter Ten

It was quieter than he'd imagined it would be. Not that he'd ever spent much time imagining the sound of a rattlesnake. But the noise itself was just a soft rattle, like a handful of beans being shaken in a coffee can.

Yet, that one quick, low sound echoed like a hammer through his chest.

He clung to the saddle, gripping the sides of the horse with his thighs as he fought to stay in the stirrups. The horse reared up again, his back feet faltering on the soft bank of the river.

"Whoa," Adam yelled, not knowing what other command to use to calm the terrified horse. He waited to feel the steady settling as the horse's feet gained purchase on the ground, but it didn't come.

Instead the horse slid backward, his back legs sinking into the water as it fell into the river, dumping Adam off its back as it struggled to swim.

The shock of the icy cold water stole his breath.

Adam fought his way to the surface while the current

tried to pull him back down. Even though he'd grown up next to the ocean, he wasn't a strong swimmer.

Panic tightened like a hard ball in his chest, threatening to freeze his limbs. His brain seemed frozen as well, and his body reacted on instinct as he tried to keep his head above water.

Blinking against the spray, he caught sight of the bank, and his alarm grew. He'd been carried into the middle of the river and had already drifted quite a ways. His horse was nowhere in sight.

Think. Focus. Swim, you idiot.

His arms flailed in the water as he tried to propel himself toward the bank. Panic warred with logic as he felt his efforts failing.

He cried out as a large mass bumped into his body, then a firm hand grabbed the back of his shirt.

"I've got you," Skye cried as she pulled him toward her, and he hauled himself over the front of her saddle.

Gasping, he clung to the horse's neck, his fingers stiff from the cold.

"Hold on." Skye guided her horse through the water. It let out a whinny as it climbed up the bank on the other side of the river.

Adam slid off the horse, stumbling to the ground and falling into the dry grass. He didn't even care about the dirt and mud covering his clothes—he was just so happy to be on dry land.

Skye dropped to the ground next to him, rubbing his arms to increase their circulation. "Are you okay? Adam?"

He blinked, trying to focus on her face, then shook his head, like a dog shakes the water from his fur. "I'm fine. Just give me a sec to catch my breath."

"What the hell happened? One minute you were plodding along behind me, the next you were in the river."

"A rattlesnake was on the path," he explained, trying to

keep his teeth from chattering. "It spooked the horse. When it reared back, we fell in the water." He lifted his head, searching the clearing for the horse, alarm filling him as he failed to see it. "What happened to him? The horse?"

"Don't worry. Horses are great swimmers," she assured him. "But it must have really been scared. It climbed back out of the river and ran for the trees. It's probably halfway back to the ranch by now."

"Ah shit. I'm sorry."

"Don't be. It's not your fault. Besides, he knows how to get back home." Her eyes cut to the cluster of clouds that had drifted over the mountains. "But we need to get to camp and get a fire built. Besides getting you warm and dry, we should get the tent set up as soon as we can, just in case those clouds decide to dump a storm on us."

He looked up at the dark clouds. "Rain? But the sun is still out." Just barely. The round fiery ball was settling behind the row of rocky peaks, slowly dipping lower even as they spoke.

"Thunderstorms crop up quickly in the mountains. And they can drop buckets of rain and bring vicious lightning." She hauled him to his feet, then got back onto her horse.

His legs were stiff as he put his foot in her stirrup and climbed on behind her. She took his hands and pulled them in front of her, wrapping his arms around her.

The warmth of her back felt amazing, but he pulled away. "I don't want to get your clothes even more wet."

She pulled his arms tighter and eased slightly back against him. "It's okay. I was in the river so my jeans are soaked anyway." She kicked her heels into the haunches of the horse. "Let's just get to camp."

• • •

Thirty minutes later, they'd made it to the camp and had their remaining supplies unloaded. Skye had tied the horse to a tree then unsaddled it, securing the saddle, bridle, and blanket under a tarp against the rocks.

She and Adam had quickly gathered enough wood and kindling to build a fire, and she snuck a glance at Adam now, as he rubbed his hands together in front of it.

His dark hair fell across his forehead, and a smudge of dirt marred his otherwise perfectly chiseled jawline. He was so cute, yet he didn't seem to realize it. He was confident in his intelligence, but she sensed he didn't have a clue how good-looking he was.

He didn't have the swagger and charm that so many of the cowboys she knew had. Including Clint. Although Clint had more than just a swagger—he had the whole good ol' boy package, from the country twang to the manners that would make a Southern mama proud. And she was sure that Clint knew he was good-looking, and he often used that fact to his advantage.

Adam knew he was smart, and it was obvious to others that he was, as well, just by the way he spoke. But he didn't make other people feel dumb. She liked that about him. She liked a lot of things about him.

Tightening her fingers, she yearned to wipe the dirt from his face and caress his cheek. His cheek, his neck, his shoulders. Hell, she just wanted to touch him. Anywhere would do.

He must have put in his contacts this morning, because she hadn't seen him wearing his glasses all day, and she kind of missed them. She'd never had a boyfriend who wore glasses before, but she liked his. She'd even fantasized about sitting on his lap and slowly taking them off, then taking everything else off, too.

Did I just say boyfriend?

She needed to get a grip. To quit thinking about the way

his wet shirt was sticking to his pecs or how cute his butt looked in those jeans. She'd be better off focusing on getting camp set up or more than his shirt was going to get soaked.

She gave him a minute to get warm as she unpacked the camping equipment, then instructed him on how to help her get the tent set up. Once their shelter for the night was standing, she hastily threw what was left of their gear inside, all while keeping an eye on the darkening sky.

Neither one said it out loud, but by the way Adam fidgeted with the ties of the tent's fly, she knew they were both very aware that his horse had ridden off with the other tent…and his sleeping bag.

They'd set up camp against the side of the bluff. This was one of her favorite places. With the view of the mountains opening up in front of them and the sound of the river behind them, it was almost magical.

If Adam wasn't swayed by the awesome wonder of nature in this place, then she should just throw in the towel now.

A drop of rain hit her cheek, and she tipped her head up to study the dense dark clouds. A low rumble of thunder sounded across the sky.

"We'd better get in the tent. The storm's almost here."

Holding the flap open, Adam crawled in, and she followed, zipping the tent door shut as another boom of thunder rolled through the air.

This one was followed by a loud crack, and the tent was lit with a quick burst of light as a bolt of lightning flashed through the sky.

Adam's eyes rounded as he ducked his head. "Holy shit. That sounded close."

"It probably was. I think the storm is going to be right on top of us. Those clouds were racing across the sky. So that means it could be bad, but it shouldn't last too long."

As if her words were a signal, the sky opened up and their

tent was hit with a barrage of rain.

"What about the horse?" Adam asked, raising his voice to be heard above the storm.

Aww. Her heart just melted a little. "He's okay. He lives outside. He can handle the rain. Did you want to bring him into the tent with us?"

"No. Of course not. I just thought…" He shrugged. "I don't know." His gaze drifted around the tent, obviously trying to avoid looking at her.

She touched his knee. "It's okay. I think it's really sweet of you to think of him. If we were at the ranch, we'd probably bring him into the barn. But he'll be okay. Horses are tough."

"Horses are bad-asses. I've never been this close to one before. I had no idea how cool they actually were. Or how big. They can do anything—run, climb, swim—all while hauling people and loads of stuff on their backs. They're awesome."

"Yeah, they are. I can't imagine my life without horses. I've been around them all forever. I even used to barrel-race when I was a teenager."

"How do you race a barrel?"

She laughed. "You don't race *against* the barrel, you race around it. A course is set up with a series of barrels, and you and your horse race around them as fast as you can. You try to get as close to them as possible without touching them or knocking them over. Whoever runs the course the fastest, wins."

"Wow. That sounds terrifying. I started to panic every time my horse broke into a trot. I can't imagine running at full speed. Did you ever win?"

She shrugged, her chest pushing out a little with pride. "Yeah, I did. I was pretty good. But that was all before Cody."

He nodded, understanding without saying anything else.

Another bolt of lightning flashed through the tent.

He cringed. "It sounds like it's getting w-w-worse." His

teeth chattered together, and his body suddenly shook with a hard shiver.

"Geez. You must be freezing. You need to get out of those wet clothes and into the sleeping bag." She dug a small lantern from her bag and hung it from a loop in the top of the tent. Flipping the switch on the side, she turned the lantern on, bathing the confines of the tent in a soft glow of light.

He nodded.

"Here, let me help," she said, after watching him struggle with his boots. "Hand me your foot." She tugged his boots off and set them by the door to the tent, then busied herself pulling off her own boots while he shimmied out of his drenched jeans.

She snuck a quick glance at him as he yanked his shirt over his head, and her mouth went dry at the sight of his lean and muscled chest. All he had left on was a snug pair of black boxer briefs. The guy was seriously sexy.

This wasn't the way she'd imagined him getting naked in front of her—and she *had* imagined it—but it would do.

Grabbing the sleeping bag, she untied it and spread it out on the floor of the tent. She unzipped one side, and her stomach swirled in anxious nerves at the soft, whispery sound of him sliding naked inside it—well, practically naked. Naked enough that it was making her skin warm as heat surged through her veins.

Her nerves were all over the place, so she focused on pulling a sweatshirt from her bag and arranging it like a pillow at the head of the sleeping bag.

But the tent was small, and he was so close, brushing against her as he tried to wiggle down into the bag. She could smell his aftershave and the scent of his shampoo. He smelled freaking amazing.

It was something different, a rich scent of musk and masculinity, and it just smelled expensive. It made her want to bury her head in his neck and inhale him.

Hell, it made her want to do more than that. She didn't just want to smell him, she wanted to touch him and taste him, to climb on top of him and run her hands over his muscled chest.

And for the first time in as long as she could remember, she wanted a man's hands on her. Not *a* man's, *this* man's. Adam's hands. She wanted to feel Adam's hands caressing her skin—feeling, touching, taking.

Her mind was going crazy with the wild thoughts, and her hand trembled as she started to zip up the side of the bag.

He set his hand on hers. "Wait. You need to get in here, too."

Her heart pounded against her chest so hard she was sure he would be able to hear it. "Me?"

"Yeah, of course." He pushed up and braced himself on his elbow. They were practically on top of each other in the crowded space, and his face was just now inches from hers. She saw his Adam's apple bob in his throat, and his voice was soft as he asked, "Aren't you wet?"

She blinked, heat rushing through her swirling belly, at the double entendre of his question.

She knew he hadn't meant it like that, but the words hung in the air, teasing them both. "My jeans *are* damp. Er, I mean, yes, I am wet. Wait—"

Avoiding his gaze, she focused on her pants, fumbling to get free of them. The sound of the zipper descending felt as loud as the crack of lightning.

He held open the flap of the sleeping bag, wordlessly inviting her in with him.

She squirmed inside, conscious of how small her black lace bikini underwear suddenly seemed, and caught her breath as their bare legs brushed against each other.

"I'm sorry I screwed up and lost the other sleeping bag

and tent," he said.

Her head rested on the crumpled sweatshirt, and she peered up at him, then dropped her gaze to his mouth. She wanted to kiss him, to be bold and press her lips to his. Even though it was a terrible idea, and she'd already come up with a hundred reasons why she shouldn't get involved with Adam Clark.

But they'd already kissed once. And it had been spectacular.

She'd forgotten how amazing a first kiss could be. How having a man's weight on top of her could feel so good. And so right.

Adam had awakened something in her that she'd tried so hard to bury. And now her body ached for his, yearned for his touch.

But what if he didn't feel the same way. What if last night had just been a fluke, a chance moment, and he'd realized, like her, that it was a bad idea. What if he was just putting up with her so he could keep warm in a freak thunderstorm?

There was only one way to find out.

He'd just said he was sorry he'd lost the other tent and sleeping bag.

She took a deep breath then spoke, her voice barely above a whisper. "I'm not."

His face remained serious, his gaze fixed steadily on hers. "I'm pretty sure your shirt got wet in the rain. I think you should take it off, too. Just in case."

A grin tugged at the corners of her lips. Damn, she did like this guy.

"Good idea. Just in case." She grabbed the hem of her shirt and pulled it over her head, reveling in the small gasp of breath she heard him take. She was glad she'd chosen the lacy bra that morning instead of one of her plain beige ones.

She laid her head back on the makeshift pillow, her

shoulder nestled in the crook of his arm.

He looked down at her, and she could feel the heat of his gaze roaming across her body. "You are magnificent."

Another grin spread across her face. She loved the way he talked, the way he used unexpected words to describe things.

Never had anyone ever called her "magnificent." And she loved it. Basked in it.

So instead of pulling the sleeping bag around and covering herself, she let him look, let him drink her in, the hunger in his eyes causing her nipples to tighten against the lacy fabric of her bra.

A shiver ran through her as he lightly rested his hand on her neck then slowly drew the backs of his fingers down her chest and across the pale edges of her breasts that spilled over the top of her bra.

His movements were slow, seductive, as if he had all the time in the world.

And he did. They had all night.

Just the two of them in a tiny tent, with the rain beating against the roof and her heart thundering in her chest, as she slowly came undone with each brush of his fingers along her skin.

She caught her breath as he slid the tips of his fingers along the lacy edge of her bra, anticipation burning through her core.

He still didn't hurry. As if he knew what delicious torture he was doling out, he dipped his thumb inside the fabric and circled the pebbled bud of her nipple.

A soft moan escaped her lips as he teased the sensitive tip.

The softest touch. A single stroke and her body felt like it was alive for the first time in years. Alive and on fire. And burning for more of his touch.

How could she have forgotten the sweet sensation that

sent surges of heat spiraling through her?

She tipped her head back, closing her eyes, and let the feelings wash through her.

He must have taken her exposed neck as an invitation, because she felt his warm breath on her skin a second before his lips settled against the soft spot below her ear.

His kisses were tender but held a note of hunger, as if he were delicately feasting on her skin. Tasting her. Savoring her.

She sank into the sensation, letting it wash over her as she clutched a handful of the slippery sleeping bag in her fist.

He laid a trail of warm kisses down her neck and across her collarbone.

Sliding his whole hand into one side of her bra, he freed her breast then cupped it in his palm. He squeezed and molded it with his hand before dipping his head and sucking the tip into his mouth.

Another moan escaped her, this one a tight sharp cry of ecstasy as he released her nipple then circled it with his tongue before taking it back between his lips.

How could he have her so worked up, and he hadn't even taken off her bra?

Another flash of lightning lit the tent, and she opened her eyes. The air itself was so charged with the combination of the storm and the sexual tension that she could almost imagine sparkles of energy shimmering around them.

What was happening to her? She didn't have thoughts like this.

She was a no-nonsense, take-charge, get-things-done kind of girl. There was one person she could count on and it was herself. She didn't have time to waste on fantasies of a knight in shining armor riding in, sweeping her up on his stallion, and kissing her senseless.

In her experience, there were no happily-ever-afters. Her prince charming had turned out to be the court jester, leaving her behind to find his own tales of adventure and other less-than-fair maidens who followed cowboys around the rodeo circuit.

And what made her think an engineer who had no idea how to even ride a stallion was going to sweep her off her feet?

Because you've never felt like this before, her heart whispered.

Because he had kissed her senseless and sent her heart into a tailspin of emotion.

Because from the minute he'd stepped off the bus and offered her that goofy grin, she hadn't stopped thinking about him.

A low rumble of thunder rolled through the air, telling her the lightning was several miles away. But the storm was still here, raging through her chest, roaring through her heart, with the charge of a lightning bolt filling her with the sizzle of electricity.

"You okay?" Adam asked, breaking through her jumble of thoughts.

She blinked, her breath ragged, her body still reeling from his touch. "Yes. I'm just…" She took a deep breath. "It's just been a long time. A long time since I've let anyone touch me like this." She lowered her gaze, unable to meet his eyes. "Since I've felt like this," she whispered.

He reached up, tilting her chin until she looked into his eyes. "I've *never* felt like this."

Oh.

She held her breath. Waiting. Waiting for him to go on.

"I know it sounds horribly cliché, but I felt something the first time I laid eyes on you. I saw you walking toward the bus, and I felt like I'd been punched in the gut. You were, you are, the most beautiful thing I've ever seen. My brain was on overload, wondering how I'd landed at a dude ranch in

Colorado, wondering if the guys were going to show up, and totally caught up in how great your butt looked in those jeans. But it was the first time I heard your laughter when we were battling that stupid bat, that I knew, at least my heart did. You smiled up at me, and I was lost. I knew you were different. Special." He shook his head. "No, extraordinary."

Extraordinary? Okay, maybe he didn't have a white stallion, but he had a silver tongue and an arsenal of beautiful language that spoke right to her heart.

"You're not saying anything. Am I just making a fool of myself here? I'm sure you have guys throwing themselves at you all the time. Do you think I'm a total idiot?"

She shook her head. "No. I don't think you're an idiot, at all. I think you're saying everything exactly right, and you're describing how I feel, too. I'm just not as good with words as you are." She touched the side of his face, resting her palm against his cheek. "I think you are…" She searched her mind for the biggest, best word she could think of. "Spectacular."

A grin broke across his face. "I'll take that."

"That's how you make me feel. Spectacular squared times infinity."

He arched an eyebrow. "Squared times infinity?"

"Okay, so maybe I'm not the best mathematician. But you know what I mean. I'm not used to this. I don't do this."

"*This?*"

She ran her finger along his bottom lip. "This. Touching. Kissing. Being with a man. I haven't done this in years. I don't let anyone get close enough."

He wrapped his leg around hers and pulled her body tighter to his. "Close like this?"

Her exposed breast pressed against his bare chest, and she sucked in a breath as she nodded.

Dipping his head, he laid a soft kiss on the corner of her lips. "And this?" he whispered against her mouth.

"Yes," she whispered back.

He leaned his forehead against hers and let out a shaky breath. "I want to touch you, to feel you. I can't think of anything I've ever wanted more. But I don't want to push you if this is too much, if you don't feel like you're ready."

Everything about this night had her feeling like she was losing control. And she wasn't sure if she liked that feeling or if it was completely freaking her out. But his words calmed her nerves and gave her the sense of security she needed.

She got to decide what happened next and how far she wanted him to go.

Another burst of lightning flashed through the tent, but the storm in her chest subsided as the steady fall of rain hit the roof of the tent, and Adam's hand tenderly caressed her cheek.

Her gaze was fixed on his—on his crystal blue eyes that looked at her with heat and hunger.

A slow bob of her head and another whispered "yes" was all she could manage before his mouth slanted across hers in a ravenous kiss.

Chapter Eleven

He deepened the kiss, his tongue sweeping across hers, and Skye felt more than heard his low growl of desire.

Then he slid his hand down her neck and across her shoulder, tugging her bra strap down the side of her arm so her other breast spilled free. His lips followed, kissing her shoulder, her chest, taking turns licking and sucking at her taut, exposed nipples.

She wanted to reach behind her back and unclasp her bra, rid her body of it, but it was almost sexier having it just pulled down, as if Adam had wanted to ravish her so fiercely that he didn't have time to even fully undress her.

His mouth continued its heavenly torture as he moved lower, kissing first her ribs then her navel.

Ripples of desire swept through her as he skimmed his tongue along the top edge of her panties, toying with her, his breath hot against her skin.

His hands slid along her waist, then down her back, then under the elastic band of her underwear. He pulled them down, the fabric skimming across her sensitive skin, then tossed them to the floor.

He knelt between her legs, his gaze sweeping across her body as he raised her arm above her head then bent forward, laying a line of hot kisses along the tender skin of her bicep, the side of her full breast, down her ribs, and across her hip bone.

Spreading her legs, he lowered his head, running his tongue along the inside of her thigh.

Anticipation swirled inside of her, like coils tightening, as her body ached with yearning. She'd forgotten this feeling of delicious torture, the wonderful torment of having an ache between her legs. She clutched the folds of the sweatshirt above her head, digging her fingers into the fabric and letting out a gasp as he laid a hot open-mouthed kiss on her center.

Ripples of pleasure tore through her body as he licked and stroked. Using his tongue and his hand, he started a slow, seductive tease, then, responding to her writhing hips and cries of pleasure, he found a fast and glorious rhythm that took her soaring. Pulse racing, she let out a moan as her body tensed then broke free, falling apart as she shattered into glorious, beautiful bliss.

She closed her eyes as she collapsed, her limbs fluid against the silky down fabric of the sleeping bag.

Feeling Adam move, she opened her eyes to see him kneeling above her, his arms braced on either side of her shoulders as his hips rested between her still trembling legs.

He leaned down, placing a tender kiss on her shoulder, and sending fresh heat surging through her veins. "You okay?"

"Yes. More than okay. Amazing."

His lips twitched in a prideful grin. "Yes. Amazing."

But she wanted more.

He was already in her heart, but she wanted to be completely filled by him.

"I wish…"

His eyes narrowed. "Wish what?"

"Nothing bad. I just wish I had come more…prepared. If you know what I mean." Although nothing could have prepared her for what had just happened.

His grin widened, and he reached for his crumpled jeans. "I do know what you mean. And I've got it covered. I was a boy scout, you know, and one of our mottos was to 'be prepared.'" He dug his wallet from his pants, then fished out a foil packet and held it up.

She gazed down at the wallet still in his hand. "Do you only have one?"

He laughed, his grin breaking across his whole face. "I'm not *that* prepared. But I like what you're thinking." His lips curved into a wicked grin, and a naughty gleam lit his eyes. "And I *am* resourceful. So I'm sure I could think of something that would suffice."

"I like what you've come up with so far." She couldn't stop her own smile. Feeling bold, she reached up to run her fingers lightly across his chest.

"Yeah?"

"Yeah."

"I've got a lot more ideas," he said with a sexy grin as he ripped the top off the foil packet.

Warmth spread through her, heating her skin. She couldn't wait to see what he thought of next.

• • •

Adam shivered, his bare skin whispering against the down sleeping bag as he pulled it tighter around his neck. Cold air bit his cheeks, and he blinked at the bright sunshine that poured into the tent as Skye peered through the flap.

"Good morning," she said, her smile almost as dazzling as the early morning sun.

He grunted in response.

She chuckled. "I've made a fire and got some coffee going. You should come out here. The sunrise is incredible."

Sunrise? What in the world were they doing up before the sun?

He wanted to snuggle back into the warmth of the sleeping bag, but she'd uttered the magic word and the allure of coffee had him reaching for his clean T-shirt.

He crawled out of the tent, dragging the sleeping bag with him. Wrapping it around his shoulders, he stood up, stretching and marveling at the view of the sun coming up over the ridge. It was pretty awesome.

Even if he was freezing in only a T-shirt and his underwear. "Why is it so damn cold? Isn't it supposed to be summer? Or did I sleep through the rest of the season?"

"It is summer. It's summer in the Rockies. It gets cold in the mountains at night."

"Good thing I have something to keep me warm." He inched closer to the fire and opened his arms as Skye held out a mug of coffee. She stepped into the circle of his arms, and he wrapped them both in the sleeping bag. Inhaling, he captured the scents of coffee, her shampoo, and pine trees.

She smiled up at him. "Not a bad way to start the day, huh?"

"Not a bad way at all." He accepted the warm mug from her and took a sip of the bitter brew. With a grimace, he swallowed then took another sip.

"We call that cowboy coffee," she explained, chuckling at his obvious distaste. "It's part of the camp-out experience."

He choked down another swallow. "It's good. I can feel the hair growing on my chest already." He glanced down at her shirt, noticing that she hadn't put her bra back on. "How about you? Has that coffee affected your chest?"

She shook her head. "I don't think so."

"Let's go back in the tent. I think we should take off your shirt, just to make sure."

Her eyes crinkled at the corners as she laughed, and his heart tumbled in his chest.

Damn, he had it bad for this woman.

Just seeing her smile was doing something to his insides. He'd thought he was just attracted to her, but now he knew it was more.

Everything in him screamed that this was a bad idea. He lived a life of logic and practicality. And there was nothing logical about falling for a cowgirl who lived not only in another state, but in a whole other world.

They had nothing in common, no shared interests, and their lives couldn't be more different. Nothing good was going to come out of this. Nothing but a broken heart.

But it was his heart, not his logic-based head, which commanded him to follow her curvy, heart-shaped butt back into the tent.

An hour later, they emerged again, the coffee in their mugs cooled and the embers of the fire graying to a smoky ash. But neither of them were cold.

They might have used their one condom the night before, but Adam was pretty inventive in coming up with alternative ways to put a smile on her face. And now, she was even more anxious to get back to the ranch where he could replenish his supply.

"As much as I'd like to spend the rest of the day out here with you, we should probably head back," she told him.

He nodded and helped her pack up their camp. She saddled her horse and tied their supplies, the rolled up tent, and the sleeping bag to the back of the saddle. Sticking her foot in the stirrup, she mounted the horse and held her hand out to him. "You're going to have to ride back with me."

He pulled himself onto the horse, settling into the saddle

behind her. He still wasn't totally comfortable on a horse, but having her butt nestled against his groin and his arms wrapped around her waist certainly made the ride more enjoyable.

His jeans were still slightly damp from the night before, but the sun offered them warmth as it shone down on them.

"The breakfast food was tied to your horse," she said, handing him a granola bar. "This will have to hold you over until we get back to the ranch."

"Good. This is just what I was in the mood for." He was actually ravenous—the night's activities had definitely built up his appetite—but it had been worth it. He unwrapped the snack bar and shoved it in his mouth.

Skye was a skilled horsewoman, and she led the mare up the river to the shallow area where they were supposed to have crossed the night before.

The ride down the mountain was easier from the back of her horse. Without the worry of having to control the animal, Adam could sit back and simply enjoy the view. "It really is beautiful up here."

"I told you. Something about the mountains seeps into your soul. Once you've had a taste of them, enjoyed their splendor, it's hard to get them out of your mind."

His heart tightened at her words. He knew she was describing the mountains, but every word described how he felt about her.

They were crossing a clearing, and the horse reared back as the brush in front of them swayed with movement. Hoof beats sounded, and a rider emerged from the trees.

A rider who looked like something out of a movie, with his starched red western shirt and white felt hat.

Adam's shoulders slumped. He knew he could never compete with the likes of Clint Carson. The cowboy was the kind of guy who belonged in Skye's world, and he obviously wanted to be there.

Clint's mouth was set in a tight line as he approached Skye's horse. "You all okay?"

Skye's back stiffened. "Of course. Why wouldn't we be? You think I can't handle a simple camp-out on my own?"

Clint's eyes narrowed, flashing Adam a stern look. "You *weren't* alone. And we got worried this morning when we saw Blaze had come back to the barn by himself. Especially since he still had a tent and a sleeping bag tied to his saddle. That must have made it a cold night for somebody."

"We managed," Skye answered, her voice as cold as the night he'd suggested.

The cowboy's gaze shifted from her to Adam and back again, as if assessing the situation. But he didn't say anything else, just turned his horse around. "I'm just glad y'all are okay. We don't usually have a horse come back without its rider."

Skye's horse fell into step behind Clint's, and they silently rode the rest of the way back to the ranch. The easy laughter was gone, and a sour taste filled the back of Adam's throat as he realized that Clint would never have lost his horse or half of their supplies.

Although, he reminded himself that given the outcome, he'd rather have shared a tent and a sleeping bag with Skye any day. Who cared about a little embarrassment?

But it still stung his ego.

His legs were stiff as he slid off the horse and held out a hand to help Skye.

She ignored his offered hand, scowling at the gesture, and swung her leg over the back of the horse then landed deftly on the ground. "I can manage on my own."

Their comfortable banter was gone. Adam wondered how much of that comment was directed at his gesture and how much at their burgeoning relationship.

Maybe *relationship* was too strong of a word.

Hell, he didn't know. All he knew right then was that he

wanted to go back to his room, take a hot shower, and put on some dry, comfortable clothes. "I guess I'll see you at lunch."

"Yeah, see ya." She offered him a lighthearted wave, but her shoulders drooped as she turned and trudged away, leading the horse into the barn.

But she didn't show up for lunch, and Adam didn't see her the rest of the afternoon.

Cody came to his room mid-afternoon and told him that Hillside, the original cabin he'd booked was clean and ready. The boy talked non-stop about the game as he helped move Adam's stuff to the cabin.

Adam listened with half an ear, nodding at Cody's ideas and agreeing with most of them, but his heart wasn't in the conversation. He couldn't figure out what happened to Skye, why she hadn't been at lunch or bothered to find him that afternoon.

Her whole countenance had changed as they rode back to the ranch that morning, as if each step brought them closer to the reality of their real lives and further from the fantasy world they'd shared up on the bluff.

He understood that. Still, he wanted to talk to her.

"Thanks, kid. See you later," he told Cody as he dropped his things onto the sofa in the cabin.

"Yeah, don't forget about the dance tonight. Everybody will be there. Even some folks from Cotton Creek are coming up for it. We've got a band and everything."

"I'm a little wiped out, but I'll think about it." He let out a sigh, not sure that he was telling the truth, as he closed the cabin door behind the boy.

He could think of any number of things he'd rather do than spend his evening awkwardly standing around a country hoe-down. Hell, he didn't even like country music. Although, he had to admit, he didn't mind the stuff they'd danced to that second day when Skye had given him lessons.

But now she'd conveniently disappeared. He was pretty sure she was avoiding him.

Well, two could play that game. If she didn't want to see him, that was fine. He'd spend the night tucked up in his new cabin and finish his book. In fact, a night in by himself sounded great.

• • •

Skye cursed as a piece of straw bit into her hand. She was setting up hay bales and trying to get the barn ready for the hoe-down that would start in a few hours, but she couldn't seem to keep her mind focused.

She should have been happy, floating on cloud nine. Hell, she'd just had great sex—amazing, toe-curling, howl-at-the-moon sex—so she should have been in a fabulous mood.

Instead, she was irritable and grumpy, and her mind was racing in a million different directions.

Last night had felt almost like a dream. When she and Adam had been up on the mountain, all alone, everything had seemed so easy, so right.

So why did things seem so *not* right now?

It had started when Clint had found them and given her a look that told her he knew exactly what she'd done the night before. Then as they got closer to the ranch, it felt like reality was setting in, and she started to question what the hell she had been doing.

It was true she hadn't had sex in years, so the fact that she'd given herself to Adam so easily—not only easily, but with reckless abandon—seemed completely out of character for her. She'd always put the ranch and Cody's needs above her own.

And hell, she'd only known this guy a few days. So what could she have been thinking?

She hadn't.

She hadn't stopped to think of the consequences at all. She'd just plowed forward, for once, letting her own needs, her own wants, come before anyone else's.

And God, she had wanted Adam. She still wanted him. Something about him made her feel like they weren't strangers, that they'd known each other forever. And it wasn't just the physical part of their relationship, although he did make her feel warm and treasured just by holding her hand.

It was also the comfortable banter between them, the easy teasing, the way he treated her as if she was smart and capable, the way he treated Cody like he really enjoyed being around her son. And the way her heart raced whenever they were in the same room. All of these things combined told her that what she was feeling for Adam was real.

They did have a connection. She knew it, could feel it.

Still, she and Adam lived in two separate states, two separate worlds. How could they ever have a future together—if he even wanted one? Maybe she was just his entertainment for the week, something to pass the time while he was stuck at an isolated dude ranch in Colorado.

She didn't think so. But how could she know for sure?

All of these thoughts muddled together in her brain, and she went back and forth, driving herself crazy, trying to figure out what she should do.

She had guarded her heart so carefully, not letting anyone get too close. How could she let herself fall for a guy who didn't even live in the same state, someone she knew was going to leave in only a few days?

What a joke. She was acting like she could stop herself from falling for him when it was already too late. She'd not only fallen, but had plunged head-long and deep in…love?

No. She couldn't say it, couldn't think it. How could she already be in love?

She needed to slow down, put the brakes on, think this through. She had a kid to consider and a ranch that was in financial trouble. Those were the things she needed to be concentrating on.

Shoving another hay bale in place, she dropped down on it, ignoring the stiff straw that poked at her legs and backside. She cradled her head in her hands, then dragged her fingers through her hair.

She knew being around Adam only clouded her already hazy judgment, so she'd avoided him all afternoon. It wasn't fair. Not to him, or to her. But she couldn't face him, couldn't think straight when she was around him, couldn't make hard decisions when he was in the same room with her. She needed some time to herself, to contemplate what she wanted to happen with them.

He was probably wondering what was going on with her.

But how could she explain her behavior, when she didn't understand it herself?

• • •

A few hours later, Adam stepped into the barn, a country beat pounding through the floor boards under his booted feet.

A band was set up in one corner of the barn, and tables laden with food covered the opposite wall. His stomach growled at the scent of BBQ sauce and grilled meat that filled the air.

A guy had to eat, right?

Couples in colorful western garb packed the dance floor, and Adam was surprised to see Josh swinging Brittany around with rhythmic ease. He was even more surprised to see her laughing and apparently having a great time as her new husband led her around the floor.

In fact, everyone seemed to be having a good time.

Skye had told him that they held a monthly barn dance in the summer and that the town of Cotton Creek was always invited. It seemed half the townspeople had accepted the invitation and shown up in their country finest. Young and old alike filled the barn, talking, laughing, and carrying plates piled high with food.

Adam's gaze swept the room, searching for a particular blond cowgirl. He wondered how she would react to seeing him.

She could have just been busy today—she did run a dude ranch, after all—but he felt like she'd purposely avoided him.

Not that he'd been looking for her or anything.

He'd just felt like taking a walk around the ranch this afternoon. And it was pure coincidence that he happened to be in the lodge and thought he'd stop by her apartment to see if he could check his email.

Cody had answered the door and explained that Skye was out. He couldn't think of an acceptable way to inquire about her whereabouts without sounding like a creeper, so he'd just let it go.

His visit wasn't completely wasted, though. The kid had let him use the internet, and he'd spent twenty minutes catching up on emails and touching base with Ryan and Brandon. At this point, it seemed unlikely that the pair would make it to Colorado.

Which was actually okay with Adam. He wasn't as keen on sharing the cabin with his two friends—especially if Skye happened to come by.

He still wasn't sure why he'd been moved out of the lodge. Had it been done purposely?

He'd have to ask Skye—if he could ever find her.

He continued to scan the crowded barn for signs of her blond head, then his heart leaped as he heard her familiar laughter.

She was standing by the drink table with Captain Cowboy, and suddenly, the sound of her laughter—knowing that it was due to something Clint had said—grated on his already tense nerves.

Why had he even come to this stupid dance?

He turned to make a quick escape before anyone saw him.

"Adam, dude. You made it."

Too late.

He sighed as he turned back and answered Josh's enthusiastic greeting. "Hi. Yep, I made it. Looks like you guys are having fun."

"Yeah, the band is great," Josh said. "And the food is amazing. You've got to try some."

Before he could protest, the younger man had already shoved a plate and some utensils in his hand. "The barbeque sauce is incredible. And the pulled pork is to die for. Everything's delicious."

Adam filled his plate, then followed Josh toward one of the picnic tables.

Another couple sat on the other side of the table, and the man held out a hand as Adam sat down.

"Wade Baker. You must be one of the guests this week."

Adam shook his hand. "Adam Clark. From California."

"Nice to meet you. I'm one of the rangers in the state park to the south of Hawk's Ridge. I come up a couple times a week and do guided hikes or programs for Skye's guests. This is my girlfriend Reese."

Adam nodded to the pretty woman sitting at Wade's side. "Nice to meet you."

"What do you do, Adam?" she asked.

"I work in the gaming industry."

"Like fish and game?"

He smiled. "No. Like video games."

"Adam's kind of a super star in the gaming world. His company designed and produced *Masters of Misfortune*," Josh said, sliding into the seat next to Adam.

"No way. I love that game," Wade replied.

"Thanks." Adam fidgeted with his fork. He just wanted to eat and get out of here.

"Wade's a certified bee keeper," Josh explained.

Brittany carried over a couple of plates filled with cookies and chocolate cake, setting them on the table before sitting down on Josh's other side. "Bees are actually kind of fascinating. I never thought of them as cool before."

Wade grinned. "I don't want to give away everything about them. I'm coming up the day after tomorrow to do a whole program on bees and native birds for all of Skye's guests."

Adam focused on his food, letting the others at the table continue their conversation, wondering how much time he needed to sit there before he could escape back to his room.

"Hey, Skye. We were just talking about you," Wade said.

Adam lifted his head to see Skye approaching the table. The roll he'd just eaten sank like a hard rock in his gut as he waited to see her reaction. He swallowed when she offered him a small smile before turning back to Wade.

"Oh yeah, well don't believe anything this guy has to say about me. Nice to see you, Reese." She leaned down to give the other woman a quick hug.

"I wasn't telling them any of *those* stories I know about you," Wade said, then offered the rest of the group a conspiratorial wink. "Not yet, at least. Skye and I went to school together, so I know a few tales about your ranch hostess. I might even share a few if someone offered to bring me a piece of cake."

"Don't you dare." Skye laughed as she gestured at Josh to sit back down. "Are you still planning to come out on Friday and do the program on bees?"

"Yeah. We were just talking about that. I have a lunch meeting that I can't miss, so I'll come out in the morning then head into town. Then I'll come back up later in the afternoon to lead the hike to the waterfall, if that works."

"That sounds great. And as long as you're going to town, I may have you pick a couple of things up for me."

Skye was doing her best to not look at Adam, but the conversation lulled, and he knew he needed to jump in if he was going to get her attention. But what the hell did he know about bees? "I think your program sounds interesting," he said. "I know I'll be there."

That got her attention. She raised an eyebrow at him. "You want to come to a program about nature?"

"Sure. I've found that I have a new appreciation for doing things outdoors."

Her eyes widened, and a tiny smile tugged at the corner of her lips. She raised a hand and pointed at his chin, and he waited for her to say something clever in return. "You've got some barbeque sauce on your face."

Oh shit.

His shoulders slumped as he grabbed a napkin from the table and wiped his face. He was batting a big fat zero and was wishing he'd just stayed in his cabin. So far, staying home to read a book had never made him feel like an idiot.

He turned to Josh. "I think I'm going to call it a night."

"What? No way, dude. The band's just starting up again."

The crowd clapped and cheered as the music started and the dance floor began to fill. Brittany hopped out of her seat and grabbed Josh's hand. "I love this song."

"Come on, you guys gotta dance," Josh called as his bride led him to the floor.

"We're in," Wade said, standing and holding out a hand for Reese.

Which left him and Skye alone at the table, staring awkwardly at the floor.

He'd already made a fool of himself, why not go for broke? "Would you like to dance?"

She hesitated. Just for a second. But he still caught it. "Yeah, sure."

"Never mind. We don't have to."

"No, I want to." She stood up and held out a hand.

His mouth was dry, and he took a quick gulp of iced tea, then pushed his glasses up his nose and took her hand.

I am a successful man and just had this woman naked and calling out my name last night, he reminded himself, trying not to look at her butt while he followed her onto the dance floor. *Be cool.*

He took her in his arms, racking his brain for the steps to the dance.

"Quick, quick, slow, slow," she reminded him, while settling into the crook of his elbow.

"Got it. Thanks." He offered her a tentative smile, and his heart lightened at the slight one he got in return. "I'm still not very good at this. I'm afraid I'm going to break your feet."

Her smile faltered. "I'm afraid you're going to break my heart," she whispered.

He pulled back, gazing down into her eyes. "Is that what this is about? Why you've been avoiding me today?" He lowered his voice to match the volume of hers. "Why you've been acting like I'm some stranger instead of the guy you just spent the night with, curled up in a sleeping bag."

She nodded. "I don't know what I was thinking. Last night, it all made sense. But as we were riding back today, it was like reality seeped in with every step we got closer to the ranch, and I realized what I had done."

"What did you do that was so bad?" His feet kept moving, but his heart felt like it was frozen in his chest as he waited for her response. Was she going to say it had been a mistake?

Was it? Probably.

They lived in different states, in different worlds. She needed someone who could be here for her, who could help her with the ranch, help her with her son. He didn't know anything about what it took to run a dude ranch, and he knew even less about how to raise a kid.

Hell, he sometimes felt like a kid himself. Memories of the last woman who'd left him filled his head. Those were pretty close to the exact words she'd used. He played games for a living, he spent too much time with his friends (who were actually his business partners, so that one hadn't seemed quite fair) and never ventured outside of his comfort zone… or outside, at all.

What was wrong with not wanting to go out all the time? He'd created a comfortable home that had all that he needed. Why would he want to leave it to go out to places that made him feel uncomfortable?

Except suddenly, he felt like there *was* something else he needed.

Some*one* else. Someone that he was willing to step out of his cozy little box for.

Someone that he was willing to go camping with, to get on a horse for, and to spend an evening feeling like a complete idiot as he tried to country dance on the stained timbers of a barn floor.

Was this all a mistake? Maybe.

But he didn't care.

Her gaze dropped to the top button of his shirt. "I like you, Adam. But…" She paused, and he held his breath, waiting for all the reasons she had for not wanting to get involved with him.

But before she could finish her sentence, a hard tap poked him on the shoulder.

"Mind if I cut in?" Clint didn't wait for an answer. Instead, he slid his hand between them and pulled Skye into his arms. "You looked like you were having trouble with the steps, Mr. Gamer Guy. Maybe you should stick to the computer, and I'll take care of Skye." He gave him a confident wink before leading Skye onto the dance floor.

What the hell? Why did she just let Clint take her from him?

He strained his neck to follow their moves. Was that a half-hearted attempt to pull away he saw, or was she simply relieved that the cowboy had saved her from having to finish her sentence? He couldn't tell.

Around Clint's shoulder, she gave him an apologetic look and mouthed, "I'm sorry."

For what, though?

Adam stood at the edge of the dance floor, feeling out of his league.

He didn't need this shit. He had a life in California—a good life. One that didn't involve dust, or cow manure, or conceited cowboys.

Turning on his boot heel, he marched out of the barn, trying not to think about the other thing that his life in California didn't have.

Skye.

• • •

Adam read the same page for the third time in a row, his thoughts too jumbled to focus on the plot of the novel.

He'd been back in his cabin for several hours but still couldn't seem to relax. He'd taken a hot shower, made a cup of tea (while wishing for a beer), tried to sleep, given up, and had spent the last twenty minutes attempting to read the book that had totally captured his interest before.

Before Skye.

He'd even tried his hand at making a fire. It didn't seem like it should have been that hard. Thick stacks of wood sat on the hearth, and he'd loaded a few pieces into the fireplace then thrown several matches on them. But they didn't catch fire, so he gave up.

Maybe he should give up on this stupid dude ranch, too. He'd come here to do research for the new game and had actually compiled pages of notes. He might not have the internet, but he could still work on his laptop, so he backed up all of his plans for the new game on a flash drive.

It felt so old school, taking notes with a pen and paper and not saving things online. In some ways, he thought it had helped his creativity, given him a new medium for getting his ideas down. And it had actually been kind of nice to not be encumbered by the constant need to keep up with social media and technology, to not be tied to his phone or constantly checking his email.

His phone had been in his bag for the last two days. The thing probably wasn't even charged. And he wasn't sure how much he really missed it.

But it didn't matter. Didn't matter if he was starting to enjoy the simpler, slower pace of life at the ranch, didn't matter that he kind of liked the smell of pine that wafted through the open windows of the cabin, or the view of the mountains every time he walked outside.

It didn't matter, because this wasn't his life. It was just a vacation from his reality.

Maybe that's all this thing with Skye was, an escape from his normal life.

Maybe once he got back to California, to his real life, he'd forget all about her.

He hoped so.

He let out a sigh and laid his head back against the chair.

Closing his eyes, he let his mind drift to Skye. To thoughts of her soft skin, the way she smelled, the way she felt naked and wrapped around him.

He was almost asleep, when he heard a soft knock on the cabin door.

Or thought he heard it. Maybe he just wished he heard it. Wished that she would knock on his door, then come in and crawl into his bed.

He crossed the room, his nerves taut with anticipation as he yanked the door open.

But no one was there.

Shit. He must have been dreaming.

He took a step outside, his gaze going automatically toward the lodge, and saw a figure walking down the path, away from his cabin.

A figure of a woman.

"Skye?"

She turned, just for a moment, and then continued to walk away.

Chapter Twelve

"Skye. Wait."

She heard Adam calling her name and his footsteps as he hurried to catch up with her. She considered the option to just keep walking, but she'd been raised with better manners than that, so she stopped, letting out a sigh as her head and shoulders slumped forward.

This had been a stupid idea. She'd been a fool to sneak out to Adam's cabin in the middle of the night.

But she couldn't help it. She'd hated the way he'd left the dance, and she hadn't been able to get him out of her mind as she'd been lying in bed, trying to sleep. She'd finally given up, decided to take a walk, and her feet had led her to his door.

The lights had been on, and, as if her body had a mind of its own, her hand had reached up and rapped softly on the door.

Relief had flooded her when he hadn't answered, and she'd tried to flee back to the lodge. He would never have to know that she had even been there.

Or at least that's what she'd thought as she'd snuck away.

Until he called her name.

"Hey, wait up," he said, catching his breath from jogging after her. He was barefoot, and the gravel had to be digging into his feet. All he wore was a pair of black shorts, and she tried to focus, her attention distracted by his lean, muscled chest.

"Sorry, I didn't mean to wake you." It was the only thing she could think of to say. She'd had seventeen other ideas rehearsed—all perfectly executed passages that would end with him inviting her in and accepting her lame apologies by taking her in his arms and then into his bed.

Okay, they hadn't all ended that way. But most of them had.

She'd been a mess all day—one minute giddy over the amazing night they'd spent together, the next chiding herself for getting involved in something she knew would never work.

"You didn't wake me. I couldn't sleep," Adam said. "I was just going to make some tea. Come in. Have a cup with me."

"Okay." She followed him back into the cabin and sat on the edge of the sofa as he grabbed cups from the cupboard and filled them with water. She glanced around the room at the discarded paperback and the logs piled haphazardly in the fireplace. "What happened here? Were you trying to start a fire?"

He chuckled as he stuck the mugs into the microwave. "*Trying* is the operative word. I'm used to fireplaces that turn on with a switch. They have fake wood and gas flames. I never knew starting an actual fire would be so hard. I probably threw twenty matches on those stupid logs, but I couldn't get any of them to burn."

"That's because you have to light the kindling first. Once it catches hold, the flames will move to the logs. But you have way too many of them in there." She pulled two chunks of wood out, then built a nest of kindling and newspapers under the remaining logs. Striking a match, she lit the kindling and blew softly on the tinder, nurturing the flames until they caught on fire.

He handed her a steaming mug, the teabag's string dangling over the side. "So that's the secret—I should have started slower then let the fire build, instead of trying to force it. I guess I just needed you." He held her gaze for an extra beat, evidently trying to make sure she got his message. Then he backed up and sank down on the sofa.

He must have turned off the kitchen light as he came in, because she suddenly noticed how dim the room was. The glow from the fire was the only light left in the room.

He patted the sofa next to him.

Sitting gingerly on the edge of the couch, she took a sip of her tea, letting the warm liquid soothe her dry throat.

He waited, patiently watching her, as he sipped his own tea.

"I'm sorry," she finally said.

"For what?"

"For everything."

"Everything? That's a pretty big apology. Are you including global warming and the Cuban Missile Crisis in there?"

She laughed—a soft chuckle, but she felt some of the tension leave her tightened shoulders. "Maybe not *everything*. But for the way I treated you today."

He eased her back into the crook of his arm, and his fingers softly kneaded her stiff neck. "So, what's going on with you? Just talk to me."

She let out a sigh, staring into the amber liquid in her cup. "I wish it was that easy. I told you that's it's been a long time since I've done this. Any of this. Last night was amazing. Incredible. The best sex of my life. But that was up on the mountain, alone in a dark tent. Today, as we headed back to the ranch, the reality of it all slammed into me, and I didn't know how to handle it."

He didn't say anything, so she kept going. "I didn't know how to face it, so I avoided it, and you, today. I know it wasn't fair, but I couldn't help it. I didn't know what to say or how to act around you, how to make you understand what I was feeling."

He still didn't say anything, and she lifted her gaze to sneak a glance at him, hoping to get a clue as to what he was thinking.

He was grinning like a fool.

"Why are you smiling like that? Didn't you hear what I said?"

"Oh, I heard. You said that last night was the best sex of your life."

A grin tugged at the corner of her lips.

How did this guy always manage to make her laugh? Even when she was being totally serious. "I told you that I don't sleep around. So before your head gets too big, you should know your competition was a horny teenage boy, a cowboy that was drunk more often than not, and a terribly awkward blind date that should have never happened."

His smile didn't waver. "I don't care. I'm still calling it a win. Score one for the computer guy—best sex of the hot cowgirl's life."

This time, she did laugh. It started as a tiny flutter in her stomach then bubbled up, and came out as a burst of laughter that wouldn't stop, that had her holding her stomach as she let out a small snort. Her tea sloshed in her cup, and she set it on the coffee table.

Adam joined in, his own laughter hearty and full.

They fell back against the sofa, his arm still around her as she tried to catch her breath. "Oh, that felt good. I haven't laughed like that in a long time."

"I'm going to try not to take it personally that your fit of giggles was initiated by a comment about my skills in—"

She held up her hand. "Stop. Don't say it. I can't breathe."

"I like to hear you laugh." He twisted a length of her hair between his fingers.

She let out a breath, butterflies replacing the laughter in her stomach. "I like that you make me laugh."

"I like pretty much everything about you," he said, his voice softening to a whisper as he laid a tender kiss on her bare shoulder.

She'd already been in bed when she'd decided to take a walk, so she'd thrown on a pair of shorts and a zip-up hoodie over her tank top and slipped her feet into a pair of sandals. As she'd leaned back, the hoodie had slipped off her shoulder, leaving Adam the perfect spot to kiss, and she caught her breath as his lips touched her skin.

A shudder ran through her, but she wasn't cold. And she wasn't about to pull the sweatshirt up. In fact, she wanted to take it off, to take everything off, as her skin heated from Adam's nearness.

"*Pretty much* everything?" she whispered back, trying to keep her tone teasing and light.

"I like your smile, and the positive way you look at life. I like the way your eyes sparkle when you talk about the ranch and your son." He turned his body to face her, lifting his hand and tracing his fingers softly down her cheek and along her chin. "I like that soft sound you make in your throat when I kiss your neck, and I love the way you smell, the way you feel."

He leaned closer, dipping his head to set a tender kiss on her neck, continuing his list in a murmur against her throat. "Your skin is so soft. And your hair. I love your hair."

She tipped her head back, closing her eyes as she surrendered to the delicious things he was doing with his lips.

His mouth moved from her neck, down across the ridges of her collarbone.

She knew she should just go with the moment, just keep her mouth shut and let this happen. But she couldn't. "What is it that you *don't* like about me?"

He lifted his head, tilting his chin to study her, as if trying to ascertain if she was serious or still teasing. "Well, I'm not exactly a fan of the way you avoided me today. And I don't like that we live in two different states."

She let out a shuddering breath. "We live in two different *worlds*."

"I know."

"Everything about our lives is the opposite of each other. We couldn't be more different."

He arched an eyebrow at her. "Don't they say opposites attract."

"The attraction isn't the problem."

"No?"

"God, no." She took in his wildly mussed hair, the dark stain of stubble along his chiseled jaw, the taut muscles of his bare chest. "When I'm around you, I can almost feel my body humming with electricity. I want you like nobody else. I want you to the very brink of distraction."

"Then we are not so different. Because I feel the same way about you. And I don't get it."

She arched an eyebrow at him.

"I mean, *I get it*. You're gorgeous, and funny, and have an amazing ass. But I don't usually act like this—all impulsive and reckless—falling for a woman I've just met and having mind-blowing sex with her in a tent in the mountains. I don't do spontaneous or wild. My life is all about practical solutions, orderly schedules, and having things in neat little boxes that make sense. Nothing about being with you makes sense. You've blown my neat little boxes all to hell. You strode into my life in your cowboy boots and snug jeans and turned everything I know on its head."

She smiled, glad to know that he was struggling with this as well. "You've blown my orderly life all to hell, too. Look at me right now—sneaking out in the middle of the night to see a man. My hands are sweating, and my heart is pounding just sitting on the sofa next to you. I'm supposed to be focused on my job, my son, this ranch. I don't have time for daydreams and fantasies about a cute guy who wears glasses and barely knows how to ride a horse."

He offered her a wicked grin. "Like what kind of fantasies?" His hand skimmed the hem of her shorts. "Like fantasies of me doing this?"

"Yes, that and more." She let out another shaky breath. "So much more."

He slid his fingers along her inner thighs, and as much as she wanted him to keep going—like *really* wanted him to keep going—the practical side of her mind cried out to be heard. She put her hand on top of his.

"But I don't know how to process all of this. This all feels like it's happening so fast. I can't catch my breath. I like you, but I don't like that I have no idea what our future holds or if we even have a future. I'm used to being in control, and when I'm around you, I seem to lose all sense of restraint."

"I hear what you're saying, and I agree that this is happening fast, but maybe this is just the way that these things happen. I've never felt like this before, either, but that doesn't mean it's wrong or that it isn't real. Because, Skye, I have to tell you, there's more that I *don't* like about you."

She swallowed. *More*?

He'd been saying everything right, everything she wanted, needed, to hear. What if this was the part where he let her down easy, where he told her all he was interested in was the physical part of their relationship? The part where he reminded her he was going back to California and that he would leave, just like she knew he would.

He picked up her hand, turned it over, and laid a soft kiss in the center of her palm. "I *don't* like that I can't seem to breathe when I'm around you, that seeing you ties my stomach in knots, and that being around you makes me nervous as hell. I consider myself a pretty smart guy, but I *don't* like that I can't seem to think straight when I'm around you. That I can't focus on anything—that I can't think about anything but you. I *don't* like that I'm leaving in a few days, because I can't imagine getting through an entire day without seeing you, talking to you, kissing you. And I don't like it when you're *not* around, when I'm not touching you."

Oh.

She didn't know what to say. No one had ever said things like that to her before. The sweetest thing Cody's dad had ever said was, "Thanks for getting me a beer."

Her chest rose and fell as she struggled to catch her breath, and her palm prickled where his lips had touched it, sending heat up her arm and through her chest.

He lifted her chin, peered into her eyes, and then dropped his gaze to her mouth as he ran his thumb lightly across her bottom lip.

The flames of the firelight flickered in his eyes, his gaze hungry and full of desire. "Maybe we're more alike than you think."

"Maybe we are." She leaned forward, resting her hand lightly on his chest, her fingers grazing over his bare skin as she kissed his neck. "Because I don't like it when I'm not touching you, either."

His body trembled as she circled his nipple with the tip of her finger, then kissed him again. She trailed her tongue down the skin of his throat and laid another kiss in the hollow at its base.

He let out a quiet moan, but she felt the vibration under her mouth. Her body responded, her own nipples tightening against the fabric of her shirt.

In her haste to leave her apartment, she hadn't bothered with a bra, and the pebbled peaks of her breasts poked through the thin cloth of her tank top as she shrugged out of her hoodie.

Adam noticed, the heat of his hungry gaze sending tendrils of fire licking through her veins as her aching nipples tightened even more.

He gripped her now bare shoulders and dragged her up to his chest, dipping his head and slanting his mouth across hers. His tongue delved between her lips, seeking to taste and devour, kissing her as if every corner of her mouth held some new secret to discover.

She kissed him back, matching his desire, kissing him until her lips tingled and her insides were hot and liquid.

He pulled her onto his lap, spreading her legs so they straddled his waist. His strong fingers dug into her hair, then stroked down her back, pulling her closer, then grasping the hem of her top and yanking it over her head.

Hot flesh pressed to hot flesh as she clung to him, digging her own fingers into the hard muscles of his back.

He picked her up, standing from the sofa with her legs still wrapped around him, and continued to kiss her as he carried into the bedroom.

Pulling back the blanket, he laid her gently on the bed, then slid his hands under her waistband and peeled her shorts and panties down her legs, leaving her naked. The sheets were cool on her heated skin.

He shimmied out of his own shorts, kicking them across the floor, then crawled onto the bed above her. Anticipation and need surged through her veins, hot as lava, pooling at her core.

Her breasts ached for his touch, and she groaned, low and husky, as he bent his head and sucked her tender nipple between his lips.

His hands moved over her, exploring, caressing, touching her with a ravenous need—she'd never felt so wanted and so cherished before.

He rose above her, grabbing a plastic sack from the nightstand next to the bed and pulling out a box of condoms. "I went to the gift shop today and got some supplies." He shrugged. "You know, just in case."

She offered him a slow, seductive grin. "I hope you got the big box."

He chuckled. "As a matter of fact, I did. I told you that I'm a pretty smart guy." He ripped open the box, pulled out a foil package, and covered himself with the contents.

This is how it's supposed to be, she thought as they laughed together. Sex was hot and steamy, but it was also supposed to be fun. So much about it was messy and awkward you had to be able to laugh about it. And be with someone that you felt comfortable laughing with.

It surprised her how comfortable—how very right—she felt when she was with Adam. Her nerves were jumpy and her stomach was sometimes in knots, but that was more out of anticipation than anything.

She was so inexperienced with all of this, but he made her feel like she was perfect. Like she was beautiful and sexy. And she loved it.

The problem was that she was pretty sure that she loved him—that she'd fallen in love with him up on the mountain. And that's probably what had scared her the most as they rode back down.

Adam settled between her legs, then leaned down to kiss her.

The feel of his lips and his warm skin against hers robbed

her of any other logical thought, and she let herself surrender to the wonderful things he was doing with his mouth and his hands.

She caught her breath as he eased into her—lost herself in the sensations of heat and pressure—right where she needed it.

Yes, there, right there.

• • •

Adam woke the next morning to the smell of coffee in the air. His body was stiff and sore, but in a good way. He'd just closed his eyes again when he heard the bedroom door creak.

"Knock, knock."

"Please let that be a naked woman holding a cup of coffee in her hands," he said, his eyes still closed.

He heard her feminine chuckle. "Close."

He cracked open one eye.

She stood next to the bed, wearing his faded engineering T-shirt, her hair in a tangled "just got out of bed after a hot night of sex" way, holding a steaming mug.

Something in his chest flipped over, and he was fairly certain it was his heart.

Although, how could he even feel his heart anymore, when he was pretty sure that last night he had given it completely to her?

He sat up, blinking, and reached for his glasses, putting them on before accepting the cup and taking a long sip. "That's good. Much better than the stuff you made on the mountain. I've never had to chew coffee before."

"Hey, you wanted the 'real western' experience, and that included crunchy coffee. And speaking of experiences, I've got your next excursion planned for this morning."

"Please tell me it includes you and me and not leaving

this bed."

She laughed. "It does include you and me, but it's not in this bed. Or this cabin. I'm going to get showered, then I'll meet you in front of the lodge in an hour. But first, I have to try to sneak back into it and act like I was just out for an early morning walk."

"Maybe you should put your own clothes back on, then."

"Good idea."

"That means you have to take *my* shirt off." He offered her a lurid grin as he peered at her over the top of his glasses. "I'm happy to help."

She giggled, then struck a seductive pose and slowly pulled the T-shirt over her head.

He caught his breath at the glorious sight of her naked body covered only by the handful of cotton she teasingly held in front of her.

Setting his coffee on the nightstand, he reached for her hand. He swallowed at the sudden emotion clogging his throat. "Skye Hawkins, you quite literally take my breath away."

She inhaled her own sharp breath, her eyes going wide at the compliment.

Then she let the T-shirt fall.

Chapter Thirteen

Two hours later, their excursion began.

Adam walked up to the lodge at nine on the dot and was surprised to see Skye sitting on a four-wheeler parked in front of the porch steps.

"No horses?"

"Nope. Just horse-power." She patted the seat behind her. "Hop on. I've already got our lunch packed. I have something I want you to see. Well, Brandon was the one who was really excited for you to see it. You can thank him for setting up this excursion."

He sent up a silent acknowledgement to his coworker as he crawled on the back of the four-wheeler and nestled his groin up against Skye's perfect backside. Then she turned over the engine, put the quad in gear, and he forgot all about Brandon.

All he could do was wrap his arms around her stomach and hold on as she gunned it. They raced out of the yard and across a pasture, then spent the next thirty minutes riding up a rocky trail and through forests before coming out in a clearing. Skye cut the engine.

She pointed her finger. "There it is."

Adam let out a low whistle. "Is that what I think it is?"

"If you think it's an old silver mine, then yes."

They climbed off the quad, and Adam stretched his legs as he walked up the dusty path toward the ancient structure set in the side of the ridge. It looked like something out of an old movie. Thick wooden timbers formed a square around a dark entrance. The only thing missing was a faded wood sign that read CAUTION above it.

"This is so cool."

"Yeah, Brandon thought so, too. In his original emails, he'd said the old mine was one of the reasons that he chose my dude ranch over some of the others. He seemed to be really excited about it."

"That's because we've got a whole section of our game that's focused on a silver mine. Can we go inside?"

She shook her head. "No. It's been boarded up for years. My dad didn't want kids messing around in it and getting hurt."

He touched the side of one of the heavy faded timbers. "You can almost feel the history coming off the wood."

"I knew you'd like it." She sat on the side of the hill next to the opening and patted the grass next to her. "If you sit here a bit and look out over the valley, you can almost imagine what it was like. The aura of mystery and hope as men went into the mine every day, hoping to strike it rich."

He dropped onto the grass next to her and followed her gaze. "Can you imagine what it would have been like traveling halfway across the country in a wagon on just a hope and a prayer that you would find this? What a life that would have been." He shook his head. "And we complain when the barista gets our specialty coffee order wrong."

She arched an eyebrow at him.

"Maybe that's just me," he said, laughing as he leaned back on his elbows. "Thanks for bringing me up here."

They spent the next half hour exploring the area around the mine. Adam even found a fossil. He tucked it in his pocket and pulled out his phone to snap a few pictures of the mine and the scenery around it. Might as well use the stupid cell phone for something—he didn't get any better reception up here than he had down at the lodge.

He grabbed Skye around the waist, holding the phone out at arm's length and snapped a selfie of the two of them grinning into the camera, with the mine in the background. Nuzzling her ear, he whispered, "I feel like I struck it rich when I met you."

"You are such a nerd," she teased, then kissed him.

A silly grin covered his face as he climbed onto the four-wheeler with her. He *was* a nerd. He'd been called one his whole life. But something about the way she said it, especially when she followed it with a kiss hot enough to melt steel, made it sound like a very good thing.

She steered them back through the trees but took a new turn-off. Within minutes, they drove into another clearing, this one with a crystal-blue lake in its center.

The lake was gorgeous, set against the backdrop of another ridge, and it sparkled in the bright summer sun.

Skye pulled up in front of a small outcropping of rocks and unloaded the blanket and small cooler that had been strapped to the back of the quad. Several tall trees sat next to the rocks, and she spread the blanket on the ground under one of them, then laid out a picnic of fried chicken, potato salad, and fluffy biscuits.

He was going to gain ten pounds this week with all this food. *But it will be worth it*, he thought as he bit into the crispy piece of chicken.

They talked and laughed as they devoured the meal and

watched small waves lap onto the beach in front of them.

Skye packed up the remains of their picnic, then stood and pulled off her T-shirt, revealing a bright red bikini top underneath. "It's hot. Let's go for a swim."

He glanced at the lake with skepticism. "I'm not much of a swimmer."

"You don't have to swim *across* it. We can just jump in and cool off." She had already pulled off her boots and shimmied out of her jeans and was walking toward the water.

Still unsure, Adam stood and tugged off his shirt. He was pretty sure the water would be ice-cold.

But the allure of following that tiny set of bikini bottoms into the water was too much, so he stripped down to his underwear and went after her.

The rocky shore scraped at his bare feet, but that pain was nothing compared to the lung-squeezing, heart-stopping chill of the lake.

Skye had already waded in and dove underwater. She came up splashing and whooping. "Come on. The water's great. And it's better once you get your head wet."

He was already in above his waist, and the water didn't seem great at all. It seemed freezing, and he was pretty sure that a fish had just brushed past his leg. Still, he'd already come this far, might as well go for broke.

He dove into the water, and the cold stole the breath from his lungs. "Holy shit, it's like ice," he yelled as his head popped above the surface.

She laughed and swam toward him, wrapping her arms around his neck. The heat of her body helped a little.

"I'd kiss you, but my lips are shiv-v-vering," he said, pulling her tighter against him. He glanced down at her bikini top and noted he wasn't the only one feeling the effects of the cold. He liked her side effects a lot better than his.

She kissed him anyway, and the contrast of her warm lips

against his mouth, the hot sun on his shoulders, and the cold water surrounding them sent a shiver down his back. But he'd never felt more alive in his life.

She pulled back, offering him a grin and a splash, then swam farther into the lake. He had no choice but to follow.

They played and splashed in the water, then lay on the warm rocks and let the sun dry them.

Feeling happy, he sat up, stretched, and smiled down at her curvy, bikini-clad body. "I have to tell you, Ms. Hawkins, you've certainly done an amazing job of swaying my opinion of the great outdoors. I had no idea what I was missing."

She chuckled. "I've only begun to show you all the wonderful things there are to see."

He knew she was talking about nature, but he heard the double meaning and knew that just being around her was pretty wonderful in itself. "Seriously, thanks for bringing me up here. This place is awesome. I'll bet the guests really love it."

"I wouldn't know. I don't usually bring anyone up here, except Cody. Some of the locals know about it, too. I do offer the excursion of having a picnic by the mine, but I thought it would be fun to eat by the lake today and take a swim. I know it's not as big as the ocean, but it has its merits."

"It's beautiful. And even more special because you don't share it with a lot of people." He teasingly nudged her leg. "I figured you brought all of your engineer boyfriends up here."

She sat up next to him, grinning as she shaded her eyes against the sun. "You're the only engineer boyfriend I've ever had."

"I guess I set myself up for that one." He chuckled, then tore a piece of grass from a crack in the rocks and twisted it between his fingers. "So, how do you feel about the idea of *having* a boyfriend, the engineering kind, or otherwise?"

He threw the question out there, trying to appear

nonchalant, but his heart was pounding as he waited for her answer.

"I'm not sure."

Hmm. Not exactly the wildly enthusiastic answer he was hoping for.

"I haven't had a boyfriend in so long I don't really remember what it's like. Why? Are you applying for the job?"

He offered her a grin. "I think I've already submitted a pretty thorough resume, but I can offer to show you more of my 'hands-on' qualifications during the next interview."

She laughed, but then her features sobered. "You know, this job isn't just a two-man team. I come as a package deal."

He nodded, matching the seriousness of her tone. "I know. And I'm good with that. I'm good with everything right now. I don't know what the hell happened this week, whether it was the mountain air, or the step away from technology, but I've felt amazing the past several days."

She peered out over the lake. "The mountains will do that to you."

He turned to her, took her chin in his hands, and turned her face toward his. "It's not just the mountains, Skye. I do love it here. I like your ranch, I really like your kid, but you're the one that's changed me this week—changed my outlook, changed my heart. I've fallen for you. Hard. And I don't want to let you go."

She rested her hand on his. "I feel the same way. But I've been down this road before. With Cody's dad. He blew into town on the rodeo circuit, swept me off my feet, and then left me behind. Just like this, it was a whirlwind romance, but then he went back to his life, to the rodeo, and he didn't look back. Especially after he found out I was pregnant. Sure, he called a few times after Cody was born, but then he got it in his head that he wasn't actually his father, that I must have been with someone else, and I never heard from him again."

His ego flared. He hated being compared in any way to this jerk. "That's bullshit. Why didn't you have a paternity test? Or sue him for child support?"

"Because it didn't matter. I knew he was the father. But if he didn't want to be, then it was his loss. Plus, I was young and stupid, and honestly, I was embarrassed and ashamed. Ashamed that I had let myself be fooled by this dumb cowboy with movie-star good looks who turned out to be an A+ asshole. I dropped out of college and came back to the ranch, vowing never to let myself be taken in by a man like that again. I put all of my focus on raising my son and making the ranch a success. And that's what I've done. Up until a few days ago, when you arrived and all of a sudden, my heart, which I'd thought had been broken beyond repair, started beating again."

He swallowed, her words touching a chord inside of him. "First of all, although I agree that this seems like a whirlwind romance, I am in no way, shape, or form like that guy. Besides the fact that I'm neither a cowboy nor an asshole, I also don't have movie-star good looks. But I do have above-average intelligence. So, I know that having the attention and affection of a woman like you is something to be treasured, not thrown away or discarded."

Tears formed on her eyelashes, but they didn't fall. She tilted her chin and pressed a soft kiss on his hand. "You're right. You're not like him. In fact, I've never met anyone like you before. And I've never felt like this before. That's what scares the hell out of me. I'm afraid to let myself care too much about you, because I'm afraid you're just going to leave."

"Skye, that *is* going to happen. I *am* going to leave."

• • •

Skye inhaled a sharp gasp of breath.

She knew it. Knew this guy was too good to be true. Knew that despite his fancy words and emotional declarations, Adam would leave, too. Just like Cody's father had done.

Pushing up from the rocks, she strode toward their blanket and grabbed her shirt.

"Skye, wait." Adam scrambled off the boulders and followed her. He grabbed the shirt from her and tossed it to the blanket, then took her hand in his and held it against his chest. "You didn't let me finish."

She tried to pull her hand away, feeling foolish in only her tiny bikini. She hadn't even worn the thing in years, usually preferring to wear her more modest tankini, but she'd taken the little red swimsuit from her drawer this morning, with Adam's reaction in mind.

Now she just felt stupid, like a young girl who was trying too hard to impress a guy that didn't want anything real with her. "You said you were going to leave. That's all I needed to hear."

"No, that's not all. Because, of course I'm going to leave. I *have* to leave. I don't live here. I live in California. I have a life there that I have to go back to." He wrapped an arm around her waist and pulled her tightly against him. "Nothing like this has ever happened to me before, and I can't explain it, or begin to understand it, but I've fallen for you. Fallen hard. And even though I have to go back, I'm leaving my heart here, with you. So you have to believe me, you have to trust that even if I leave, I'll come back. Come back to you."

Her chest tightened, and she couldn't breathe. Her heart felt like it was being squeezed into a knot.

Could she trust him? Could she trust any man?

Her mind struggled to think, to analyze what he'd said, then he kissed her, and she lost all ability to reason. Because it wasn't just a kiss—he captured her mouth in a full-on assault. He held her to him, tight against his bare chest, and she felt not just his passion, but his emotion, as he dug his hands into her still-damp hair and growled a moan against her lips.

His movements were fast and hard—yanking the ties of her bikini loose and freeing her breasts as he ripped the tiny top from her body and tossed it to the ground.

Her nipples puckered in anticipation as he filled his palms with her breasts. He bent his knees, dipping his head to take one of the tight hard tips into his mouth.

But this was no slow seduction.

His mouth feasted on her body while his fingers fondled and touched. He fell to his knees, nuzzling his head against her waist and nipping at her hip, then stripped her bikini bottoms down her legs. His strong hands were everywhere, touching, stroking, teasing.

She gripped handfuls of his hair when he pushed her legs apart and pressed his lips to her soft flesh.

He pulled her down onto the blanket with him, continuing his passionate assault, and feasting on her body with the appetite of a starving man.

Her arms pressed out, pushing against the ground. She writhed in pleasure, grasping the blanket in her fists, arching her back to give him more.

Nothing else mattered, only this moment, with this man.

She let out a moan, a husky sound from deep in her throat, as she surrendered to him, body and soul.

• • •

An hour later, they were packed up and headed back to the ranch, Adam's arms comfortably wrapped around Skye's waist while they bounced along the trail.

The newlyweds had booked their own excursion for the afternoon, and Skye was scheduled to take them on a hike at two. She needed a few minutes to change clothes and check on Cody before she met Brittany and Josh.

Except for the hum of the quad's motor, the ride back was quiet, and she used the time to think about everything Adam had said that morning.

He'd told her that he was falling for her, but had he ever really said that he wanted to have a future with her? He'd said for her to trust that he was coming back, but how could she put all of her trust in a guy she'd only met a few days ago?

She knew she was in deep. Heck, she'd just spent the last hour rolling around naked on a blanket with him—something she could never have imagined herself doing.

But she'd done several things the past few days that she couldn't have imagined herself doing—and one of them was falling in love.

Chapter Fourteen

Adam turned to his laptop, thankful to have a few hours with the internet to get some work done. Skye had just left to take the newlyweds on a guided hike, but she'd told him to stay and use her office—and the internet connection—while she was gone.

He had just opened his email when Cody rushed through the apartment and into his bedroom. He emerged a few seconds later, a jacket in his hands. "Where's my mom?"

"She's doing a hike with Josh and Brittany."

"Shit. Er…I mean, crap." The kid's cheeks colored. "Sorry. I just needed to talk to her. When will she be back?"

"Not sure," Adam muttered, his attention focused on the long list of new emails filling his inbox.

"Shit."

This time, he tore his concentration from his work and looked up as the boy flung himself onto the sofa. "That's two shits in a row. Anything I can do to help?"

Cody sat up. "Yeah, actually there is. We get a grocery delivery on Thursdays, and I told my mom that I'd stick around to let the delivery guy in and put all of the groceries away. But Haylee wants me to take her on a hike up to the ridge. Are you gonna be around? Can you let the guy in? And just put the cold stuff away? I can do the rest when I get back."

Adam shrugged. "Sure. I'll be here for another few hours. But are you sure your mom will be okay with it?" Something about the way Cody was fidgeting gave Adam the sense that something was not quite right. He tried to think of something parental to ask. "Are her parents going with you?" Yeah, that was a good one.

"Uh, yeah. Of course. And we'll only be gone like an hour. Just tell my mom I'll be back, and make sure you let those guys in to deliver the food. And don't forget to put the cold stuff in the fridge and the frozen stuff in the freezer. I'll leave the door open so you can hear them come in." Then Cody was up and out the door.

Something felt a little off about this situation. But surely Cody knew his mom and what she allowed better than Adam did.

A semi-urgent email caught Adam's attention, and his mind switched back into work-mode as his fingers flew across the keyboard.

He dealt with that email then moved through the rest, answering, discarding, and dealing with issues happening at the company.

A door slammed, startling Adam, and Skye's voice yelled down the hallway. "Cody Hawkins!"

Adam stood and stretched his arms over his head, his back aching from bending over the laptop. He missed his ergonomic chair and keyboard that he had set up in his own office.

He stepped out of the room as Skye stomped into the apartment. "Have you seen Cody? He was supposed to meet the delivery guy and let him into the kitchen. I just walked into the lodge and there's melted ice cream and three bags of steaks bleeding out on the dining room table."

"Oh shit."

"'Oh shit' what?"

"That's my fault. I was supposed to meet him."

"You? Why? What happened to Cody?"

"I told him I would. He said he wanted to do something, and I told him I'd take care of the delivery guy, but I must not have heard him."

"Why would you do that? The Thursday grocery delivery is part of Cody's job. I *pay* him to meet the guy and get all of the food put up."

"I-I didn't know," he stammered.

"Of course you didn't. Because you don't have mounting bills that are threatening to ruin you. I can't afford to lose five-hundred-dollars' worth of groceries. And you don't have a kid that you already spent thirty minutes arguing with this morning. You have no idea what it's like to try to raise a kid on your own. But I do."

Whoa. She was really mad.

He held up his hands in surrender. "You're right. And this is my fault. But I can fix it. I'll pay for another grocery delivery."

She rolled her eyes and planted her fists on her hips. "You can't fix everything with money. Or maybe you can. I wouldn't know. But that's not what I'm trying to teach my son. I'm trying to teach him some responsibility, that if you're given a job, you're expected to do it."

"I totally agree."

"So what was so freaking important that he bailed out on his obligations?"

"He said he was going on a hike with the Hendersons."

"Well, that's a load of crap. The Hendersons were on the hike with me."

A feeling of dread started at the pit of his stomach. "*All* of them?"

"No, just Mr. and Mrs. Henderson. They said that Haylee had a headache and was staying in the cabin to read or sleep or whatever it is that teenage girls do."

It seemed that what teenage girls "did" was lie to their parents and sneak off with the cute boy whose mother was about to be even more royally pissed off.

"Well, about that. All I know is that Cody came through here an hour or so ago and said he was going on a hike with Haylee and her family. He asked me to watch for the delivery guy. And I said I would."

"And you just let him go? Without asking me?"

"I didn't *let* him do anything. All I did was agree to watch for the delivery. I didn't know he was doing anything wrong. But my guess is that he must have snuck off with Haylee while her parents were out with you. He said he'd be back in an hour, though, so I'm sure they'll be back any minute."

"When was he here?"

Adam shrugged. "I'm not sure, exactly. I didn't look at the clock. But it wasn't that long after you left, so it must have been around two."

Her face paled. "Adam, it's almost five. Are you telling me he's been gone this whole time?"

He looked at his watch, shocked to see that close to three hours had gone by since he'd opened his laptop. "I had no idea it was so late."

She pulled her radio from her pocket. "Cody Hawkins, where are you?"

No answer.

She depressed the mic button again, offering him a steely glare. "Come in, Cody."

Still no answer.

"Shit." She shook her head, then pressed the mic again.

"Anybody seen Cody?"

The radio squawked as Cal replied, "Not this afternoon. Do you need something?"

"He apparently took the Henderson girl on a hike and said he'd be back in an hour. It's been close to…" She looked up at Adam for confirmation. "You're sure?" she mouthed.

He winced as he nodded and cautiously held up three fingers. Her eyes narrowed, and she spoke through gritted teeth. "…going on three hours now. And he's not answering his radio."

"I'll take a look around for him. They should be getting back soon, though. Looks like there's a pretty good thunderstorm coming over the mountain."

"I'm sorry, Skye, I didn't know."

"You didn't know that two kids shouldn't be going on a hike by themselves? Or you didn't know that you probably should have alerted someone when they didn't come back for three hours." Her eyes flashed with anger as she marched across the room and yanked a raincoat off a hook by the door.

"Either. I'll admit I wasn't paying attention to the time, but he told me he was going to be with her parents."

"And you believed him?"

"Why wouldn't I?"

"Because you're not a parent."

Ouch. Her words stung, and not just because of the venomous way they were slung at him. It was the added meaning behind them.

He *wasn't* a parent. He didn't know anything about kids. Except for his memories of being one.

She blew out a breath and dragged her hands through her hair. "I can't do this. There are too many crazy things happening in my life right now, and I'm at my wits' end. Ruined groceries might not be a big deal to you, and maybe they wouldn't be to me on a normal day. But today is not normal. This week, this last month, too many things have been going on. I can't keep everything straight, and I'm afraid I'm going to completely lose it. I just need things to slow down and give me a chance to breathe. I can't take one more bad thing happening."

The tremble in her voice tore at his heart. "Everything's going to be okay. I'm sure Cody's fine. Any minute, he's going to walk in the door. You'll see." He took a cautious step toward her, but she held up her hand.

"Don't. I know you're trying to help, but if you take another step closer, I might break. I've only been thinking of myself the last few days, and I need to focus on my son right now. I just need to know he's okay."

He backed off, trying to give her the space she needed, understanding that her emotions were not all aimed at him but at the mounting stress she'd recently been under. She was obviously at her breaking point, and he didn't want to make things worse.

But he hated doing nothing, hated just standing there watching her try to hold it together. Her hands shook as she tightly clutched the radio. He had to look away.

Her radio beeped, and Cal's voice filled the room. "I just made the rounds, and the kids haven't made it back yet. Somebody saw them heading toward the west ridge. I'll get the horses ready so we can head up there to look for them."

Skye's eyes widened. "Oh God. What if they're lost up there? Or worse, what if one of them is hurt?"

"Don't think like that." He couldn't do it, couldn't just stand here. He crossed the room, opening his arms to offer her support, but she shook her head and took a step back.

"Of course, I think like that. I'm a mother."

His arms dropped to his sides. "I want to help."

Her voice held no emotion as she shoved her arms into the sleeves of her jacket. "I think you've done enough already."

The radio beeped again, but this time the voice wasn't

Cal's. "Hey, Skye. I heard about Cody. I'm heading over. Don't worry. We'll find him."

Oh great. Cowboy Clint to the rescue.

He fucked up by letting the kid go off into the mountains by himself, and then Clint gets to come in and be the hero by finding them.

"There has to be a way I can help," Adam tried again.

She sighed. "You can't. The trail up to the ridge is too steep to drive up, so we're going to have to ride. You'd only slow us down."

"Maybe he has his cell phone."

"The reception's terrible, especially on the mountain. But he usually carries it around, so it's worth try." She grabbed the wall phone and punched in a number, then slammed it down. "It went straight to voicemail. The only thing to do is ride up and try to find them."

"Give me his number. I can keep trying. And I can radio you if I hear from them."

She narrowed her eyes at him, as if determining if he could be trusted with the task, then gave him a quick nod and scribbled a number down on the back of an envelope sitting on the counter. "Fine. There's another radio in the office. It works like a walkie-talkie. We use channel nine."

"Skye—" he started to say, but she didn't give him a chance to finish his sentence.

Instead, she turned and walked out the door, slamming it shut behind her.

He racked his brain, trying to think of some way to help. Should he call the police? Skye hadn't suggested that, so maybe not.

What would the police do anyway? Set up a search and rescue team?

That's it. An idea popped into his head, and he raced to his laptop to open a chat box and send an urgent message to a few of his employees.

He might not be able to ride a horse, but he had a whole team of brilliant computer minds on his staff. And some of the best hackers.

It took one of his guys about four minutes to hack into Cody's phone and pinpoint the coordinates of where he was. Or at least, where the phone was. Another one had found the spot on Google maps and emailed him a photo that showed a clear picture of the section of mountains behind the ranch, with a pin in the most likely spot that the phone could be found.

Adam quickly printed out the picture and raced out of the lodge and toward the barn.

Skye was nowhere to be seen, but Clint and another cowboy were just about to ride out. Adam waved him down. "Where's Skye?"

"She's gone. She and Cal already headed up the trail."

Shit. He gritted his teeth. He had no choice but to trust Cowboy Clint.

He passed him the paper. "Do you see that red balloon in the middle of the page? Do you know where that is?"

Clint offered him a snide sneer. "Red balloon? I don't have time to look at this crap. I need to help Skye find her kid."

This guy really did not like him. He'd never seen him act like this around other people. It had to be jealousy over his relationship with Skye. But they had to put that aside now, had to focus on finding Cody.

Adam held the paper higher. "That's what I'm trying to do, too. I had my guys hack into his cell phone, and this map pinpoints pretty close to where he is."

The cowboy scoffed but snatched the paper from his hands and studied the map. "Yeah, I know where this is. It's the outcropping of boulders by Elephant Rock."

Adam lifted the radio to his lips, but Clint beat him to it. "Skye, come in. Ride toward the outcropping of boulders by Elephant Rock. I think that's where he is."

The radio crackled, and Adam held his breath, praying that she heard the message.

He let out a sigh of relief as her voice came through the speaker. "Got it. We'll head that way."

Clint answered before Adam had a chance to say anything. "I'm right behind you. Buck and I will meet you there." He crammed the paper inside his jacket and gestured to the other cowboy to follow him. Giving his horse a good kick to the side, he galloped out of the yard and into the trees, leaving Adam standing in the dust.

Feeling sick to his stomach, he glanced at the dark clouds that were moving swiftly across the sky and sent up a silent prayer that the rain would hold off.

But the first drop had already fallen, and with a roll of thunder, the sky opened up. Adam was soaked by the time he got back to the lodge.

Josh was standing on the porch when he ran up the steps. "Hey, dude. Do you think Skye has any shaving cream in the gift shop? Apparently Brit's been using mine, and I'm out." He must have noticed the stress on Adam's face, because his easy smile fell. "Hey, what's wrong?"

Adam yanked open the door of the lodge and stomped in, running his hands through his wet hair.

Think. Think.

What could he do to help Skye? To help Cody? He was sure the kid was fine. They probably lost track of time. But what the hell did he know?

Something felt off about this whole afternoon. And now, with the storm setting in, he was getting a bad feeling.

"I screwed up." He sighed and filled Josh in on what had happened.

"I'm sure they're okay," Josh reassured him. "They probably started making out and lost track of time."

"You're probably right. But I couldn't say that to Skye. And I have this bad feeling in my gut that something's wrong. But I can't do a damn thing about it. I just want to do something, anything, to help."

Josh pointed to the bags of groceries still on the table in the dining hall. "Let's start with cleaning up that mess."

"Yeah, good plan."

They salvaged what they could and trashed what had already melted or was ruined. Adam grabbed a new T-shirt from the gift shop and some shaving cream for Josh, and pushed a fifty-dollar bill through the slot of the cash register.

After changing into the dry shirt, he called the number on the side of one of the grocery bags, told them what happened, and arranged for them to deliver a duplicate order within the next hour. He gave them his credit card to cover the cost of both orders and offered to pay extra for the inconvenience of driving it up, but the woman on the phone said it wasn't necessary. She'd known Skye since she was a little girl and just hoped that Cody was okay.

She assured him that they'd have the food there as soon as they could.

Adam shook his head, not used to seeing such concern and caring in a community. Small towns. Crazy.

He couldn't think of a single place in his city that would offer to make a special delivery, after five, and required a drive up the mountains in the rain. Especially not one that didn't cost a fortune in "convenience fees."

He'd make sure he tipped the guy making the drive well.

Skye had a small kitchen staff, and they were already working on the evening meal.

Brittany had come down to the lodge, looking for Josh, and between the two of them, they worked with the staff to figure out what needed to be done to prepare the dining hall for that night's dinner.

The young couple worked tirelessly, and Brittany ran a hand encouragingly over Adam's arm as she passed him. "It's going to be fine. They'll find them."

Setting out forks and napkins wasn't much, but it gave him something to do, something to occupy his racing mind while they waited.

They'd just finished the last table when the doors to the lodge burst open, and the Hendersons came rushing in.

Mrs. Henderson's hair plastered to her worried face. "We just heard that Haylee was missing. We thought she was here watching movies with Cody."

"They aren't missing," Adam assured them. *We just don't know exactly where they are right now.* "Skye and Cal are headed up to get them."

"What kind of place are they running here?" Mr. Henderson's voice boomed through the dining hall.

"Now, honey, I'm sure everything's going to be fine," Mrs. Henderson assured him, but the tremble in her voice gave away her concern. She brushed her wet bangs from her creased forehead. "Can you tell us what you know so far?"

Adam held out a chair for her to sit in, trying to keep his own voice steady and not betray his anxiousness. The last thing Skye needed was to have irate guests who would complain about the ranch, or worse, request their money back.

He filled them in, giving them as much information as he knew.

"I knew something was up this afternoon," Mrs. Henderson said. "She was acting funny, and it didn't seem like she even had a headache. I just thought she was trying to get out of going on a hike."

The radio in Adam's pocket squawked, and Skye's voice broke into the room. "We've got 'em. We found the kids. They were right by Elephant Rock."

"Are they okay?"

"Yeah, they're fine. Cody fell, but he's okay. We think he's sprained his ankle. Haylee's fine. Just a little scared. And they're both cold and wet."

"Do you need me to call a doctor?"

"No, not yet. We're almost down. Can you call the Hendersons and let them know Haylee's okay?"

"They're here with me now. We're at the lodge."

"Okay, we'll be there soon."

Mrs. Henderson broke into tears as she wrapped her arms around her husband. "She's okay."

Fifteen minutes later, a cold draft swept into the lodge as the front doors opened and the bedraggled group stepped inside.

Clint and Skye strode in first, with the kids nestled between them. Skye had her arm around Cody's shoulders as he limped beside her. Rain dripped from Haylee's hair as she shivered, looking small and young as she huddled inside of Clint's jacket.

The other cowboys followed in their wake, knocking mud from their boots as they crossed the front porch mat, and shaking the rain off of them like a pack of dogs.

Mrs. Henderson rushed forward, her arms open, and Haylee collapsed into them, breaking into tears and sobbing her apologies. Her mother patted her wet hair. "Shh. It's all right, now. We're just glad you're okay."

Adam had a feeling the yelling would probably happen later. From all of the parents. But for now, everyone was just happy to have the kids back home and safe.

Including him.

Cody offered him a wry grin. He shrugged as he mouthed the word, "Sorry."

Adam shrugged back.

Clint strode into the dining hall as if he owned the place, setting his hat on the table and using a folded napkin to wipe the water from his hair. Adam hated to admit that he looked like some kind of Western superhero with his shirt wet and stuck to his muscled chest.

The problem was that he was acting that way, too, basking in the glory of saving the day.

Mr. Henderson grabbed his hand, pumping it in appreciation. "We can't thank you enough for finding them." He turned to Skye. "You, too. We're so grateful."

"It wasn't me. Clint was the real hero," she said, as she helped Cody ease into the dining room chair. "I still don't know how he knew to look up by Elephant Rock, but I'm glad he did. We'd already set out to search in an entirely different area."

Buck, the other cowboy that had ridden with Clint, raised his head and looked at Adam. "Actually, it was— "

"It was the least I could do," Clint said, stepping in front of the cowboy and cutting off what he was going to say.

Nice. Real nice.

He was the one who found them, but Clint got to take all of the credit. And got to relish in the adoring look that Skye was giving him for finding her lost kid.

But what was he supposed to do? He'd look like an asshole if he stepped up now and tried to set the record straight. Hell, he couldn't even blame the other cowboy for not saying anything. Clint was his boss.

Besides, what did it really matter who found them? As long as they were safe.

The staff came out of the kitchen, carrying trays of hot tea, and Brittany passed around the steaming mugs to the kids and the grateful rescue team.

Adam made his way over to Cody as Skye talked to the Hendersons.

"Hey, kid. Glad you're okay." He nudged his elbow against Cody's arm.

The preteen winced. Not able to look Adam in the eye, he kept his gaze focused on the cup of tea he held in his hands. "Sorry I lied to you. But Haylee said she liked to rock climb, and I knew this great place. I just really wanted to impress her, you know."

The boy's voice was soft, and Adam knelt next to his chair. "I totally get it, dude. I just wish you hadn't lied to me."

"I know. Me, too. I really am sorry. For everything."

Adam lowered his voice even more, and added a conspiratorial tone. "Was it worth it?"

Cody's head jerked up, and he narrowed his eyes at Adam.

Adam winked, and the boy's lips curled into a grin. He nodded. "Yeah, it was worth it."

"Why don't you leave the kid alone?" Clint's voice was hard as steel as he stepped up to Cody's chair. "Haven't you done enough already?"

Heat burned Adam's neck, and he curled his hands into fists. Not like he would really go through with punching the other guy, though he was really tempted. Then again, Clint looked like he'd have no trouble handling himself in a bar room brawl. Even if Adam decided to throw a punch, he doubted he'd come out on the winning end of that fight.

No, it was easier to walk away—to go back to his cabin—than to stand around and watch Clint soak up the accolades for finding the kids.

He slipped out of the dining hall as the rest of the group was sitting down to eat. Even though he tried not to, he listened for the sound of Skye's boot heels, following him.

But all he heard was the sound of the rain as he pushed open the doors of the lodge and made a run for his cabin.

• • •

Almost an hour had passed when Adam heard a knock on his cabin door. His heart leaped, hoping it was Skye.

He'd come back and taken a hot shower, then changed into a pair of sweats and a fresh T-shirt. Using Skye's advice, he'd built a halfway decent fire.

He set down the stupid paperback he still couldn't seem to concentrate on and rehearsed what he would say to her as he crossed the room to open the door.

But it wasn't Skye.

Chapter Fifteen

Adam let out a sigh and held the door open for Josh, who held up a foil-wrapped plate. "I saw you duck out earlier and figured you'd be hungry."

His stomach growled at the scent of food as he took the plate and peeled back the foil. Piles of barbequed pulled pork spilled out of a crusty bun. Adam lifted the sandwich to his lips and took a greedy bite. "Thanks. You're a damn good guy," he said around a mouthful of pork.

"No problem."

"So, is she still mad?"

"Oh yeah."

"Like how mad is she?"

"Pretty mad. Or at least, it seems that way from my limited experience with women. But that tight-lipped, sharp-eyed, wrinkled-forehead look usually spells trouble in my world. And that's what Skye looked like all through dinner. Cody just sat quietly, picking at his food and sneaking furtive glances at his mom and the girl."

"Poor kid." Adam let out a soft chuckle. "I feel for him.

How's his ankle?"

"I think he's going to be okay. According to him, they just lost track of time. When they were ready to head back, he slipped on the rocks, and that's when he got hurt. I guess Haylee had found some branches and they were building him a make-shift crutch to use when Skye and Cal rode up."

"Smart. Are they taking him to the doctor?"

"I guess not. Not tonight, anyway. Apparently Cal used to be a veterinarian, before he retired. He took a look at it and declared it a sprain."

Adam shook his head. *Small towns. What a different world.*

"I better get going. Brittany already went back to the cabin, and she's waiting for me. I just wanted to drop off some food for you. Are you going to that program on bees in the morning?"

He shrugged. "Maybe."

"I think it sounds cool. Hope I see you there. Take it easy, man." Josh offered him a fist bump as he headed for the door.

Adam didn't know that was still a thing. But he bumped his fist anyway. The guy had brought him a sandwich, after all.

After Josh left, he finished eating, cleaned up, and camped out on the sofa again, hoping Skye would eventually show up.

He gave up around midnight and finally went to bed, although he spent a restless night tossing and turning as he tried to decide what to do.

Should he send her a note? Show up at her door and demand to talk to her? His first thought had been to send some apology flowers—that was something he could usually accomplish in seconds online with minimal effort. But nothing at Hawkin's Ridge ever seemed to be accomplished with minimal effort.

He considered picking her a bouquet of wildflowers but wasn't sure where she'd be in the morning or if that would be considered too cliché.

In the end, he decided that actions spoke louder than words—he was going to follow through on his original plan for the day. He would show her that he cared about her by keeping his word and his end of the bargain.

He was up with the sun, already restless to get started. He showered and dressed in his normal clothes—shorts, T-shirt, and Converse—forgoing the cowboy boots and leaving them in the bedroom closet. He cleaned up the cabin, emptied his bag and his backpack, and took them with him as he locked up and headed out to find Ranger Wade.

Wade was loading his truck as Adam approached and offered him a wave. "Hey Wade, are you still heading down to Cotton Creek this morning? Can I bum a ride into town with you?"

"Sure. Hop in."

Adam climbed in the truck, wondering if he should have left Skye a note.

"You leaving?" Wade asked, gesturing to his bags.

"No, I had my staff ship some computer equipment to me, and I got an email yesterday saying a bunch of boxes had arrived at the Cotton Creek post office. I just brought these to carry it all in. Do you mind if I catch a ride back to the ranch with you this afternoon?"

"'Course. But what do you need computer equipment for? Aren't you leaving tomorrow anyway?"

"I hope not. I haven't cleared it with Skye yet, but I'd like to stay another week or so. And the equipment isn't for me. It's for Skye and Cody—new computers and routers to update the ranch's antiquated system. Have you seen what she's been using?"

"You mean that huge thing that still takes floppy disks?"

Adam chuckled. "That's the one. At least she doesn't have a dial-up modem."

The truck bounced along the dirt road as Adam detailed

his plan to update her system and add wifi to more areas of the camp.

"Sounds awesome. And expensive," Wade said. "And Skye's gonna let you do all of that for her? Are you sure?"

Adam shrugged. "I'm fairly sure. We worked out a trade, of sorts. This stuff is easy for me to do, and all of the equipment is used, so, though it seems like a lot, it's really like a tax write-off for me."

"That's why you're going to all the trouble? For a tax write-off of a charitable donation to a dude ranch?"

He picked at a loose seam on the hem of his shorts. "That, and because I've apparently fallen for the woman who runs the ranch."

"Nah, really?"

"Is it that obvious?"

Wade chuckled. "You mean by the way you stare after her like a lovesick pup. Nah. I'm sure nobody noticed."

Adam let out a heavy sigh. "That's awesome."

"Don't worry about it. You're not the first guy to fall for our Skye. She's gorgeous, inside and out. But you're the first one that I've seen her interested in. I've known Skye since we were kids. We grew up together, and I haven't seen her like this in a long time. She's a good person, generous to a fault, but she doesn't trust easily. Especially when it comes to men."

"You don't have to tell me," Adam said with another sigh, then perked up as he realized what Wade had just said. He'd grown up with Skye. "Wait. Could you tell me everything you know about this woman? Because I am going crazy trying to figure her out."

Wade's laughter filled the cab of the truck.

• • •

There turned out to be six boxes in all at the post office, and

Wade helped him load them into the truck.

"I need to go, but I'll meet you back here in a couple of hours." Wade gestured to the downtown area of Cotton Creek. "Everything's pretty much in walking distance. Grocery, drugstore, bank, and hardware store on the corner. The diner serves a great cheeseburger, and make sure you get a piece of Anita's apple pie. It's to die for."

"Apple pie sounds good, but what I really need is wifi."

"They've got that, too."

Adam patted his bag. He'd grabbed his computer on the way out the door. "Then I'm good. I brought my laptop, and I've got plenty of work to do. I'll run a couple of errands here in town, then grab some lunch and wait for you at the diner. Take your time. I'm in no rush."

Adam wandered down the main street of Cotton Creek. He stopped in at the café and got a pastry and a latte, then walked down to the hardware store and stocked up on all of the cables and accessories he'd need to get Skye's equipment up and running.

He ducked into the bank to use the ATM and saw Clint Carson in what appeared to be a heated conversation with one of the bank officers.

Hmm. Wonder what that's all about.

It wouldn't hurt to get a little closer.

Sitting down in one of the chairs outside the office, he listened in as he leaned forward, pretending to tie his shoe.

"I know the loan is due, Hal," Clint was saying. "And I told you that I've got a plan in place. I just need a little more time."

"I wouldn't call waiting for Skye Hawkins to marry you and combine your properties much of a plan, Clint."

Marry him? What the hell?

"It's gonna happen. It makes perfect sense. We've known each other since we were kids, and our dads always wanted this. I just need a little more time to get her to come around to my way of thinking. The Hawkins land covers that whole ridge. Once we combine our properties, we could easily sell off several hundred acres and still have plenty for ourselves. And that's just one idea I have. She doesn't have a clue what kind of a cash cow she's sitting on. It makes good business sense for us to merge our assets, and Skye isn't stupid. She'll listen to reason. I know for a fact that dude ranch of hers is in dire financial straits. The last few 'accidents' around the ranch have cost her a pretty penny, and she won't be able to dig herself out if another setback was to accidentally occur."

"I'm going to pretend I didn't hear that."

Clint chuckled, but in an "evil villain rubbing his hands together" way. "She's getting close to breaking, Hal. I can feel it. It won't be long before she comes running to me to save her."

"Yeah, little does she know that she'll be the one saving you."

"Can I help you with something, sir?"

Adam looked up to see one of the bank tellers standing in front of him. "Uh, no. I already used the ATM. I just had a knot in my shoelace, but I'm good. Thanks." He grabbed his bags and hurried out of the bank, hoping that Clint hadn't seen him.

That prick.

He knew that guy was up to no good.

Unfortunately, Clint had Skye completely fooled. She really believed that guy was her friend. With friends like him, she didn't need enemies.

He thought back to the day they'd repaired the fence. He'd thought it had been cut. Had Clint been responsible for that? Was that another one of his attempts to sabotage the ranch?

Who knew what this guy was capable of?

He did know that he wasn't going to let him hurt Skye again. Not on his watch.

Fuming, he crossed the street and pushed through the doors of the diner. A waitress showed him to a booth in the back where he ordered a cheeseburger and fries, then set up his laptop and got to work.

• • •

Skye nonchalantly walked past Adam's cabin for the third time that morning. Where was he?

He hadn't shown up for breakfast, and he hadn't been at Wade's program—not that she was looking for him.

Who was she kidding? Of course she was looking for him.

She'd lain awake half the night rehearsing what she'd say to him. But now, she couldn't find the guy to tell him what she'd planned.

Although, at this point, she still hadn't decided which speech she was going to give him. The one where she told him they were just too different, that although this had been fun, they should just part as friends now before one of them got hurt? Or the one where she told him that it didn't matter that they came from two different worlds, because she was in love with him and they'd figure out a way to make it work.

She wasn't sure she'd be able to deliver that second one. She'd only just admitted to herself that she was in love with the guy—she didn't know if she was ready to admit it to him, too.

Although, as it turned out, she wouldn't have to.

Because after she'd finally worked up the nerve to knock on his door, he hadn't answered.

"I hope you're not lookin' for Adam," Cal said as he walked by with a load of firewood for one of the other cabins.

"Why not?"

"Because he already left?"

"Left? What do you mean? How could he have left?"

"I saw him get in the truck with Wade this morning. He had his bags with him, so I figured he must have checked out early. I thought you knew."

"No, I didn't know." Her heart sank as she bent to look through the windows of his cabin. She didn't see any of his stuff—his paperback wasn't tossed on the sofa or sitting on the edge of the coffee table and his sneakers weren't lying by the door.

He left?

How could he have left?

Without even saying good-bye? Without even trying to work out what had happened with them the night before?

This didn't make sense. Not after everything he'd said to her. Not after all the promises he'd made.

But she'd heard promises before. And in her experience, promises were made to be broken.

Maybe he left a message with someone at the lodge.

She hurried back and checked in with everyone on the staff, discreetly inquiring if anyone had left her a note, but there was nothing.

He'd really left.

Just like she knew he would. Like she'd been afraid of, since the day she'd let herself get involved with him.

She sucked in her breath as she hurried to the barn. She needed to go for a ride, needed to get the hell out of there before anyone saw her break.

Cinching the saddle, she yanked the stirrup down then climbed on her horse and took off across the pasture at a gallop.

Holding in a sob, she pushed the horse harder, faster. The wind dried the tears that streamed down her face.

Her heart was broken. Not just broken, but shattered into

a million tiny pieces.

How could she have trusted him? Believed in him?

He was just like every other man in her life, cutting and running as soon as things got tough. It was true, they'd had a fight. She might have said some hurtful things, but she didn't think he'd leave.

Or did she?

In her heart of hearts, had she suspected this would happen all along? Is that why she got so mad? So he'd have the out he needed to leave?

Or had she been unwittingly testing him? Trying to get him to go, but secretly wishing he'd stay.

She leaned forward on her horse, holding on as it navigated up the steep path. She trusted the animal to be there for her, to stay sure-footed and keep her secure—all the things that she'd trusted Adam to do.

At least she knew the horse wouldn't let her down.

• • •

Adam passed Cody another cable. "Plug that one into the back of that router box," he instructed from under Skye's desk.

The two had been hard at work setting up the new system for the last few hours.

Adam had hoped to find Skye as soon as he and Wade returned to the ranch, but she wasn't anywhere around.

He found Cody in the barn, who'd told him that he'd seen Skye ride off about fifteen minutes before. Her horse was still missing, so Adam had enlisted Cody's help in getting the computers carried in and the new equipment in place.

He told himself that maybe it was good she hadn't been there. That this way, he could surprise her when she got back.

And with her gone, it gave him time to hang out with

Cody, and to run all of the ideas he'd been working on by him. The boy's face had lit with excitement over Adam's plans.

"That sounds so cool. I can't wait. And I know it will help the ranch. Mom is gonna freak," Cody said.

"Yeah, I'm a little worried about that. I don't want her to think I'm overstepping."

"What? No way. We came up with a lot of this stuff together, so if she's going to be upset, she'll have to be mad at me, too. But dude, she's not gonna be mad. We worked out these cool ideas to help all of us—you, me, and Mom. We'll all get something out of it."

He loved that Cody took ownership of their ideas and saw their new plans as something they'd both contributed to. That was the idea. "I just don't want it to feel like I'm steamrolling over your mom, or you. I don't want her to feel like I'm taking over."

"You're not. I helped come up with some of this stuff, and I want to help you put it together. I want us to work on it all together—Mom, too."

Skye would love that.

The kid's enthusiasm was contagious, and Adam's heart warmed. He really liked Cody. The boy was funny and smart, and they had a good time just hanging out together.

He was often uncomfortable around other people's kids, not quite knowing what to say or do. But he didn't feel like that with Cody. He was totally at ease, comfortable talking or just working next to him in companionable silence.

He knew that any future he might have with Skye included Cody, and that was fine with him. He'd spent a lot of time thinking about what he wanted his future to look like, how he could configure a life split between two states that would make them all happy.

The plans he and Cody had come up with concerning the ranch and the new game could do just that.

But he also didn't want either Skye or her son to see his plans as self-serving. He wasn't just thinking of how his ideas would help him and his company. He truly had Skye and Cody's best interests at heart. He really wanted this thing to succeed for *them.*

Thinking about it now, he realized he wanted this for Skye, wanted to help her, regardless of whether she wanted him in her life.

He *wanted* to be there—wanted that more than anything he'd ever wanted before—but he also wanted her to be happy. And he wanted Cody to be taken care of.

If Skye agreed and let him implement the plans that he and Cody had come up with, it could set them up financially for a long time. And that made it all worth it.

He just wanted this woman—this wonderful woman that had blown into his life and thrown his whole world upside down—to be happy.

Whether she wanted him or not.

But he sure as hell hoped she did. He hoped his selfless efforts showed through, that she could see that he was willing to do whatever it took to secure a future for them.

"You know, if we do this thing, I'm going to be around a lot more," he said, testing the waters to see how Cody felt about that. He didn't want to completely jump the gun. Just because he liked the kid, that didn't necessarily mean those feelings were reciprocated.

The boy picked up a set of cords and strapped them together the way Adam had taught him. "I know. That's cool with me."

Well, there you go. A smile tugged at the corner of his lips, and he turned away so the kid wouldn't see him grinning like a fool and think he was an idiot.

The gnawing feeling in his gut eased. He'd crossed the first hurdle.

Cody loved his ideas and wanted him around. Now he just had to get Skye's approval. He could only hope she'd buy in to all of their ideas.

In fact, he was a little worried that she wouldn't go for all the electronics they had set up. He hadn't realized how much stuff there was until he started unpacking it all. He'd fired off an email to his assistant with a quick layout of the ranch, telling her to go into the stockroom and just send what she thought they would need.

And his assistant hadn't left anything out. She'd sent up a couple of PC's for Skye's office and the reception area, and included laptops for both Cody and Skye. She'd even thrown in a few desk organizers.

With Cody's tools and his eager willingness to help, they spent the next few hours running cable and Ethernet cords and installing wireless routers. Now, Skye's apartment, the reception desk, and the main guest areas of the lodge all had access to wifi.

Adam was cleaning up the boxes in Skye's office when she walked in the door.

"What's all this?"

"Isn't it awesome?" Cody said. "We've been working all afternoon. Wait till you see all the new cool stuff."

"Who's we? Cody, where did all of this stuff come from?"

"From Adam."

"Surprise," he said, as he stepped out of her office. But the surprise was on him. Instead of excited shock and enthusiasm, he was met with chilly indifference.

"What are you doing here?"

"I'm setting up the computer equipment. Like we talked about." He spoke slowly, sensing that a firestorm was simmering behind her narrowed eyes.

"I mean what are you doing *here*? At the ranch. I was told that you left."

"I did leave. I hitched a ride into town with Wade to pick all of this up. I got an email yesterday saying that it had been delivered to the Cotton Creek post office."

Damn. He knew he should have left a note.

"But Cal said he saw you take your bags. And I looked in the cabin and your stuff was gone."

"Well then, you didn't look very hard. Because my clothes are still in the dresser and my toothbrush is sitting on the sink. I emptied out my bags and took them with me so I'd have something to carry all of these boxes in."

Her brows knit together, as if she was having trouble processing all of this information. "Then you didn't leave?" she said softly, almost as if asking herself.

"No, of course not. I wouldn't do that." He crossed the room and held out his arms to give her a hug, but she took a step back. Just like she'd done the night before.

Patience.

He didn't know a lot about animals, but he knew enough to understand that you had to use caution when approaching a particularly skittish one. And Skye was acting as skittish as a caged dog. Her eyes were wide and unfocused, and she kept shaking her head slowly, as if engaging in some internal debate.

"Cody, would you mind giving me and your mom a few minutes?"

The boy looked to his mom for confirmation. When she nodded, he shrugged, then went into his room and shut the door.

Even though he wanted to pull her into his arms, Adam leaned on the corner of the sofa, trying to give her the space she needed. "Talk to me. What's going on?"

"I thought you were gone—that you'd left. I've spent the afternoon nursing my broken heart and writing you out of my life."

Yeah, he really should have left a note.

"Skye, I'm still here. I'm not going anywhere."

"But you are. You already said you were going back to California. I thought I could do this. I thought I was strong enough. But I'm just not. This afternoon, I thought I might actually be having a heart attack, the pain in my chest hurt that bad. I was so sure that you'd left, because that's what the men in my life do, and this afternoon, I suffered as if you had left. I don't think I can go through that again. I don't think I want to."

"What are you saying?"

"I'm saying that I can't handle losing you again. That I can't risk putting my heart out there again. I can't take it. I'd rather be alone."

"You don't mean that."

"I do." Her voice was soft and held so much misery that it tore at his own heart. "I think you should just go. The camp ends tomorrow anyway, so you can go back to California and forget that we ever met."

"I could not and will not ever forget you. And I don't want to." He took a step toward her, but she cringed, hugging her arms around her middle, and his heart broke in two.

"Just go," she whispered.

Bewildered and heartbroken, he crossed the room. She just needed some time. That was all. He just needed to give her some space.

He pulled open the door, but then turned back. "I need to tell you something before I go. I was in the bank today, and I overheard Clint talking to the banker about a loan Clint had coming due. Clint assured him that he was working on a plan—a plan to marry you and merge your properties, then sell off a portion of your land."

She shook her head. "Marry me? Sell off my land? What are you talking about?"

"That's what Clint said. And he also mentioned that some of the financial setbacks you've had lately might not have been 'accidents.' He told the banker that he had plans for another one, something that would send you running straight to him to rescue you. It sounds to me like he's in even more financial trouble than you are."

"You're wrong. You must not have heard him correctly. I don't need anyone to rescue me. And there's no way Clint would do that to me. He's my friend."

"Skye. I know what I heard. You may think he's your friend, but he's not. He's using the friendship between your fathers and the fact that you grew up together to get you to turn to him. But believe me when I tell you, he doesn't care about you, or Cody. He's only interested in getting his hands on your property. He told the banker that he had other plans for this place."

Tears filled her eyes. "I don't believe you. Why are you saying these things? I've known Clint all of my life. I've known you less than a week. Why should I believe you?"

He took a deep breath, his chest aching, terrified at what he was about to say, but unable to stop himself. "Because I love you, and he doesn't."

A sob tore from her throat, and she sunk to the floor, her knees collapsing under her.

He reached for her, but she shook her head. "Just go."

He hesitated. His heart ached to pick her up, cradle her in his lap, brush back the tendrils of hair that were clinging to the tears on her face.

"GO!" she yelled.

Emotion clogging his throat, he turned and pulled the door shut behind him.

Chapter Sixteen

Skye curled into a ball on the floor, hugging her arms around her knees as she cried. She wanted to sob, to wail, to let out the sorrowful beast that was filling her chest with pain.

But she didn't want to scare Cody. Didn't want him to see her like this. Because he was the one who mattered—the one she needed to be strong for.

She took a deep breath and pushed up off the floor. Swiping the tears from her cheeks with the back of her hand, she dragged herself into the bathroom and splashed cold water onto her face.

She took a hard look at herself in the mirror. Dark rings of mascara smudged her red-rimmed eyes, and her hair hung in loose strands around her face. She evidently was not one of those pretty criers.

She wet a washcloth and held it to her eyes, then used it to wipe away the smeared makeup as she replayed what Adam had said in her head.

What the hell was he talking about? Clint may have wanted more of a relationship, but he'd always been her friend. He'd always been there for her. Hadn't he? Especially in the last few years, when things at the ranch had started to take a turn for the worse.

She tried to think back to the things that had happened—could they have been acts of deliberate sabotage? Racking her brain, she tried to think of when her financial downturn had started.

It was after her dad had died, and she was trying to keep the place going on her own. The first accident had been an electrical fire that had burned one of the cabins down. But surely Clint couldn't have been responsible for that. He wouldn't.

She tried to recall the other things—there'd been that whole section of fence that had been destroyed in what they'd thought was a storm, and one of the sturdy ranch trucks broke down after being dependable for years. She'd had a rash of sick cattle that the vet had attributed to some type of weed or moldy hay that they might have ingested.

The more she thought about it, the more she realized that any of those things could have been caused by someone with malicious intent.

But would Clint really do that? She couldn't believe it.

There was only one way to find out.

Grabbing a hairbrush from the drawer, she yanked it through her hair and pulled it up into a high ponytail. Tucking in her shirt, she strode from the bathroom, yelling at Cody. "I'm heading over to Clint's. Be back in a bit."

"See ya," he yelled back, without bothering to open the door.

• • •

Skye's temper was still high as she marched up Clint's porch steps and banged on his door.

His ranch hand, Buck, walked around the side of the house. "Hey, Skye. Something I can help you with?"

"Hey, Buck. I'm lookin' for Clint. Is he around?"

"Sure, he's just putting out some hay for the horses. He'll be back in a few." He gestured to the front door. "Go on in and make yourself at home. I'll go tell him you're here."

He took a few steps toward the barn then stopped and turned back. "You know, there's something that's been bothering me, and I think I need to get it off my chest."

"Okay."

"It's about that computer fella that you've got staying there. The one that Clint calls Mr. Gamer Guy or something."

She rolled her eyes and let out a sigh. "You mean Adam Clark?"

"Yeah, that's his name, I think. Well, you know last night when Clint told you to head up to Elephant Rock to find Cody, and everyone was so amazed that he knew where to look for the kids?"

"Yeah."

He lowered his voice and squinted toward the barn, apparently wanting to make sure no one else was listening. "Well, if you ever tell Clint I told you, I'll deny it, but it wasn't him that knew where to look for Cody. It was that Clark fella."

"Adam? How would he even know about Elephant Rock?"

"I'm not sure exactly, but he said he had his staff hack Cody's phone's GPS or something. And he handed Clint a map with the spot marked and asked him if he knew where it was. Clint recognized Elephant Rock and radioed you before that other guy had a chance to tell you himself."

Her mind was spinning. Adam was the one responsible for finding the kids? "But he didn't say anything. He just let Clint take all the credit."

Buck pushed a hand under his hat brim and scratched his

head. "I know. That's what's been buggin' me. He seems like a fairly decent guy—like all that mattered to him was that we found those kids. It didn't seem right that he was gettin' the short end of the stick, when it was him that really found Cody and that girl."

She opened then closed her mouth. She didn't know what to say.

"I've been debatin' if I should tell you or not, but the fact that you showed up like this here tonight made me feel like I needed to speak up."

"I'm glad you did. And don't worry. I won't tell anyone that you told me."

"I'd appreciate it." He tipped a finger to his hat. "I'll go find Clint for ya."

Her thoughts were a jumbled mess as she pushed open the front door and stepped into the living room that was almost as familiar as her own. This house had been like a second home to her growing up, and Miss Martha, Clint's mama, had been like the mother that she'd always wished she'd had.

She and Clint had both lost their parents at too young an age, and that grief had reinforced their bond of friendship.

Or so she'd thought.

Had he been playing her all along? She couldn't believe it.

Her mouth was suddenly dry, and she crossed the room, heading for the sink to get a glass of water.

Passing the den on the way to the kitchen, she slowed and peered into the room. He'd seen the stack of unpaid bills in her office. Maybe he had a similar stack on his desk.

After glancing out the front windows and not seeing any sign of Clint, she slipped into his den. A large desk sat in the middle of the room, and Skye walked behind it, running her fingers across the piles of mail and file folders strewn across the top.

A folded topographical map caught her eye, and she pulled it out from underneath a manila folder. Unfolding the map, she gaped at what she saw.

All of the property belonging to both her and Clint had been combined and outlined in red marker. Segments of the land around the edges—of *her* property—had been shaded in light blue and marked with property value and estimated sale prices.

She shook her head, trying to comprehend what she was seeing, trying to come up with another solution, a plausible explanation that would make some kind of sense.

She couldn't breathe. Her pulse pounded through the vein in her neck as her teeth ground together.

This couldn't be right. He couldn't be planning to sell off part of *her* land.

Not Clint. He was her friend. She trusted him. He wouldn't do this to her.

Would he?

The front door opened with a *bang*, and Skye let out a yelp and almost dropped the map.

"Hey there, sugar," Clint called, offering her a flirty grin as he stepped into the office. "What brings you to my house?" His smile fell as he saw the map clutched in her hands.

"Don't *sugar* me. What the hell is this?"

Please have a good explanation.

"I wish you hadn't seen that."

That was not the response she was hoping for. "Yeah, I'll bet not."

Her hands curled into fists as her bewilderment quickly changed to anger.

"Now, don't go getting all upset. I'm sure it's not what you think."

She raised an eyebrow at him and planted one fist on her hip. "Oh really? It's not? I realize I'm just a poor helpless female, but it certainly appears to be an outline of portions of *my* land that you are apparently planning to sell."

"All right, simmer down. I was hoping to present this idea to you in a different setting, like maybe with some candlelight, a little mood music, some champagne, and a pretty little diamond ring."

"A diamond ring?" she sputtered. Holy shit. Adam had been right. About everything.

Stop it. She couldn't think about Adam right now. She needed to focus on the task at hand, the task of bringing Clint Carson to his dirty-rotten, filthy knees.

"Come on now. Surely this can't come as too much of a surprise to you. You know that I've always had a thing for you, and our dads had been talking about us getting together for years. It just makes sense. Besides being a sound business decision that's mutually beneficial to us both, we'd be a great match. We have so much in common. Hell, we practically grew up in the same house."

"Not exactly, because evidently my daddy raised me better than yours did."

"Now, Skye, there's no call for that."

"Oh yes, there is. There is exactly a call for that. Because if you think for one minute that I would ever marry a cheating, lying, double-crossing back-stabber like you, you've got another think coming. When, and if, I ever get married, it will not be because it's a sound business decision. Especially one that is so clearly one-sided."

"Skye, you're just being emotional now. If you'd just calm down and think about this rationally, you'd see that this could help both of us. You know I've always cared about you, and merging our properties could save us both."

If I could just calm down and think rationally? Had he really just said that?

Her nails dug into the insides of her palms, and she could

practically feel her blood boiling beneath her skin. Crumpling the map into a ball, she threw it on the desk. "That's what I think of your smart business decision. And if you think you are ever going to get your hands on my land, you are sorely mistaken. I have no intention of selling any of my land now, or ever. You will never get your slimy hands on me or my property."

She turned on her heel and strode from the room, calling over her shoulder, "And you can take your smart business decision and stuff it."

• • •

The nerve of that guy, she thought as she let herself back into her apartment. Her hands were still shaking.

"Hey, Mom," Cody said, coming out of his room with a laptop in his hands. His easy smile fell when he saw her face. "What's wrong?"

"Me—" She'd started to say "men" then caught herself, since Cody was one of them. She didn't want him to feel like she was negative toward *all* men…just those dirty snakes who tried to use her.

She amended what she was going to say. "Many things. Many, many." She slumped onto the sofa, patting the seat next to her. "Come sit with me a minute. I could use a friend."

"You're kind of weird, Mom," Cody said, but he plopped onto the couch next to her.

"What's with the laptop? Who'd you borrow that from?"

"I didn't borrow it from anyone. It's mine."

She laughed. "Yours? Where did *you* get a laptop? Did I miss the Computer Fairy? Was she here earlier, doling out random computers to the whole ranch?"

"No, just to you and me. And the Computer Fairy isn't a *she*, it's a *he*. It's Adam."

"Adam gave you that laptop?"

"Yeah, of course. Mom, don't you remember seeing all those boxes when you came in before. We told you we'd been working all afternoon. Come on, I'll show you." He stood up and led her toward her office.

She realized, for the first time, that the apartment had been cleaned up. The empty boxes and plastic wrap that had been strewn around before were gone. Adam must have cleaned it all up before he left.

Stepping into her office, she let out a gasp.

She didn't even recognize her own desk.

It was the same desk, in the same place it had been that morning, but it looked completely different. Her old clunky computer was gone, replaced with a sleek new monitor and keyboard. Her paperwork and envelopes were neatly arranged in desk organizers, and a bright yellow cup that read "Good morning, Sunshine" held all of her pens and markers.

Everything had been dusted and neatly arranged. The floor had even been vacuumed. And a petite vase holding an array of wildflowers sat to the left of the monitor.

She shook her head, unable to believe it. "Did you do all of this? Or did Adam?"

A grin broke across her son's face. "We did it together. Adam worked on setting up all of the computer stuff, but he said he didn't want to mess with your mail and paperwork, so I organized all of that. I mean, I didn't read everything, but I grouped all of the ranch stuff together and filed it by categories, like activities, guest stuff, and lodge stuff. You can look at it and see what you think."

"I think it's incredible. I can't believe you did this. For me."

"Well, *we* did it. And Adam did most of it. Like that cup is totally from him. And the flowers. And it was his idea to vacuum. Oh, and check this out." He tapped the space bar, and the monitor sprang to life.

Tears filled her eyes as the monitor lit, and a slideshow of pictures crossed the screen. The first was a picture of her and Cody from when he was about four—the same framed picture that was on the wall in the hallway. The second picture was the selfie she and Adam had taken at the lake.

A bubble of laughter burst from her throat as the third picture appeared. It was of Adam and Cody making goofy smiling faces at the camera. They were wearing the same clothes they had on today, so they must have a taken a selfie that afternoon.

"Do you like it?" Cody asked softly.

She wrapped an arm around her son's shoulder, her heart full to bursting. "Yes. I do. I like it very much. In fact, I love it." Tipping her head, she dropped a quick kiss on Cody's head. "Thank you."

"It wasn't all me. It was Adam, too. He's a good guy, Mom. I really like him."

Yeah, I really like him, too.

That was the problem.

The pain in her heart flared up.

Why had he done all of this? She'd treated him terribly—screamed at him, even. She'd practically called him a liar and told him to get out of her life, and he'd responded by doing all of this for her. By spending the whole afternoon setting her business up for success and picking her flowers.

She didn't understand. She'd never met a man like him before. And she didn't know whether to laugh or cry. Or both.

"There's more." Cody grabbed a slim silver laptop from the shelf. "This is for you."

She turned the computer over in her hands, marveling at its sleekness. "This is too much. We can't accept all of this."

"Mom, we have to. It's really going to help the ranch. Plus, we're going to need these to help with the game."

"What game?"

"The new *Misfortune.* We're calling it *Gaming and Grit.*"

"Cody, what are you talking about? What the heck is *Gaming and Grits*?"

"Not grits. Grit—you know like toughness. And it's our new game idea."

"Whose?"

"Mine and Adam's. And yours, too, I guess. At least your name's on the contract, too."

"Contract?"

"Haven't you been paying attention at all, Mom? All this time that we've been talking to Adam about the game and giving him ideas, he's been taking our ideas and using our suggestions for his new game. He said he didn't want to take our ideas for free, so he's crediting us on the game and giving us some royalties." He pulled a green folder from the organizer, opened it, and took out a stapled pack of papers. "He gave us a contract and everything. I filed it in a folder labeled 'Contracts.'"

Taking the paper, she stared down at it, dumb-founded. Was Adam really offering them a contract with royalties? For a few silly suggestions?

Her delight in the desk, and the cup, and the flowers, and the pictures—*oh my gosh*, the pictures were so amazing—was quickly turning to irritation. Adam had crossed one too many lines.

Who does this guy think he is?

"Don't you think this is awesome?"

"I think it's something, all right. And I think I need to have a serious talk with Mr. Clark."

• • •

Adam had just stepped out of the shower when he heard the

knocking on his door, pounding actually.

"Adam? Are you in there?"

Skye?

"Hold on. I'm coming," he yelled toward the door as he tugged on a pair of shorts. He was still rubbing the towel over his hair as he yanked the door open.

He was hoping she would show up, was hoping that all of his efforts that afternoon had shown her the way he felt, and that his actions spoke louder than his words. He was hoping she'd knock on his door and throw herself happily into his arms.

But she didn't look happy—no, not happy at all. In fact, by the narrow squint of her eyes and the tight set of her mouth, he would say she looked like one pissed-off cowgirl.

She slapped a stack of papers against his chest, her expression faltering for just a moment as her hand touched his bare skin. But she recovered quickly, yanking her hand back. "Just what in the hell are you trying to pull, mister?"

"Pull? What are you talking about?"

"What I'm talking about is this *thing*—this contract, apparently. What kind of game are you trying to play?"

Wow, this woman had really had a number pulled on her. She really didn't trust anyone.

He sighed. "Why don't you come in and sit down?

"Why don't you tell me what's going on?"

"Skye. Come on."

"Fine." She stepped through the door, and the scent of her surrounded him and almost brought him to his knees. He wanted to reach out, to grab her and pull her into his arms, but he was a smart guy, and something told him she *might* not be quite ready for that.

She sat gingerly on the edge of the sofa, and he dropped his wet towel on the coffee table and sat down in the chair next to hers, their knees almost touching, but not quite.

He reached for her hand, but she pulled it back, hugging her arms around her middle as if trying to protect herself.

Protecting herself from him? That thought was like a punch to the gut.

He settled back in the chair, trying to set a relaxed tone. He could feel the tension rolling off of her in waves, and he knew he needed to stay calm and not push her away.

"You want some tea, or coffee, or some water or something?"

"No, Adam. I don't want some tea. I want you to tell me what's going on."

He held his hands up in surrender. "Okay, okay. So, I've spent a lot of time thinking about you, obviously, and about us, and about how we keep talking about how different we are. But I don't want our differences to define us, or to come between us, so I devised a plan that would incorporate our differences—make them work together and complement each other. You know, so our differences seem like a positive instead of a negative."

"I don't see how *our* differences have anything to do with this." She held up the papers.

"I'm getting to that. I thought about each of our strengths and how we could combine those strengths to help both of us. Then I remembered something Cody had said that first night we all played video games together, and I came up with the idea for *Gaming and Grit*. I'm pretty proud of that name, too. It describes the concept, as well as the two of us, like I'm the 'gaming' and you're the 'grit' part." He grinned at her, but she wasn't smiling back. Not even a little. "But grit in the good sense, of course, like tough and western."

She raised an eyebrow, but her mouth stayed set in a tight line.

"Anyway, we can change the name if you'd like, but I wanted to have an idea that would use the best of what we both do. So I came up with the idea to use real settings from Hawkins Ridge in the new *Misfortunes* game, then create a camp, here at the ranch, where kids can spend a week and actually experience those settings. There could be hands-on activities that mirror what's happening in the game, for instance, a cattle drive along the same ridge that's pictured on the screen, or we could even open up part of the mine for spelunking or gold-panning. We have tons of ideas of things we could do."

"Who's *we*?"

"Me and Cody. We've been working on this all week. That kid is smart and ridiculously inventive. He's come up with some really cool ideas. He has experience with the game, so he comes at it from the participant side. Then I try to incorporate his ideas into the design from the business side."

"Wait. Cody has been helping you with all of this?"

"Yeah, of course. That's why I'm offering him, and you, a percentage of royalties. Otherwise, it would feel like I'm just stealing ideas from a kid. I wanted to talk to you about it yesterday, because you might want to set up some kind of trust or something for his future. And regardless of whether or not you decide to incorporate the ranch into the deal, I'm still using his ideas, and yours, in the new *Misfortune* game. That's the part I had the contract drawn up for. We can figure the rest of it all out later."

She rubbed her hand across her forehead. "Slow down. You're talking about contracts and trusts and incorporating the ranch, and I can't keep up."

"You're right. I'm sorry. I'm just so excited about it. And I want you to be excited, too. This is going to save the ranch. You won't have to worry about money anymore."

Her eyes widened, then narrowed, and she pushed up from the sofa. "I'm not a poor, weak woman who's searching for a man to rescue her. I don't need you, or anyone else, to *save* me."

He stood, reaching for her hand. "That came out wrong. That's not what I'm trying to do. Dammit, Skye, you've got to quit comparing me to the other men in your life. I'm nothing like them. I won't run out on you like your ex, and I won't try to swindle you like Clint. I know you don't believe me about that, but it's true."

She let out a sigh. "I do believe you. You were right, about Clint, about everything you said about him. I went to confront him and found the evidence myself. I think you may have been right about him sabotaging the ranch."

"That sucks. I'm sorry." Even though he wasn't, not really. He was sorry that she'd been hurt, and he'd make sure that Cowboy Clint paid for hurting her, but he was glad that she now saw the guy for the ass-wipe he was.

"Me, too. But I'd rather know the truth than have him continue to use me and the relationship we had for his own personal gain."

Adam jerked back as if he'd been slapped. "Do you think that's what I'm doing?"

She shook her head. "I don't know. I don't know what to think anymore."

He took a deep breath, trying to rein in his own emotions, and see things from her side. Even though his plans would benefit him, there was no selfish intent involved. In fact, when it came to her, all he could think of was what he could give to her.

And what she needed right now was patience and understanding and to know that he was in this thing for the long run. That he wasn't leaving, or trying to use or trick her.

"I know that you've been hurt before, but that's not what I'm trying to do. I promise. And I told you before that I keep my promises. Please, just give me a chance to explain. Just listen."

She slowly eased back down on the side of the sofa, but her shoulders stayed tense, her back rigid, her expression wary.

He knelt in front of her, resting his hands lightly on her knees. He hadn't planned to talk to her like this—he wished he was wearing a shirt, at least—but it didn't matter. All that mattered was that she listened.

"Please give me a chance here. And try to listen with your heart, and know that everything I'm saying is because I want what's best for you, me, and Cody—for our future together. Because that's what I want most of all, a future with you and Cody in my life. Okay?"

She nodded, not saying anything, but the tension in her shoulders eased a bit.

"I know that you are a strong, proud woman, and I admire that in you. And I know that you would never accept charity or let someone come in and take over what has been in your family for decades. So know, first of all, that that's not what I'm suggesting. This isn't charity or a handout. It's not something I'm giving to you because I feel sorry for you. It's something we would do together. I want to enter into a partnership with you, something we can agree on jointly, that will benefit all of us *and* the ranch. And it's a really good idea. I think you're truly going to love some of the stuff we came up with.

"Like, for instance, I know you said you were struggling to connect with Cody because all he wanted to do was play games. So we came up with the idea of having a week where the parents and kids would come to camp together. The parents would learn how to play the video game and connect with them. And both kids and adults would have the added benefit of spending time in this beautiful place, acting out the game. Doesn't that sound cool?"

"Yeah, it does. But I run a dude ranch. It sounds like you're suggesting we change the very fiber of the ranch into some commercialized live-action video game."

He shook his head. "No, not at all. I love the charm of the ranch, and I don't want to change that. I'm suggesting that we do three or four of these specialized camps next summer in between your regular schedule. They would be something truly unique, something that gamers have never had a chance to experience. I think you could charge more for those camps, and they would fill quickly."

"But just trying to prepare for all of that and making the changes would be incredibly expensive. I don't even have wifi."

He grinned. "You do now. That's another thing Cody and I did this afternoon. But that doesn't matter right now, because that's the beauty of the partnership. We each have something to bring to the table, Skye. I have plenty of money, so I can cover the finances. But I have no idea how to run a camp or handle guests or deal with food prep or camp-outs or even people in general. I get hives if I have to spend too much time with strangers, making small talk. So that's why I need you. You know how to do all of those things. And you're *good* at them."

She offered him a small smile, and his heart soared.

He was making progress.

"It would take both of us, *all* of us, working together. And I'd have to be on site for a lot of it, so I could split my time between here and California. And you and Cody could come out and spend time with me. So, while everyone here is freezing, you could be lying on the beach in that cute little red bikini. Doesn't that sound good?"

Her grin broadened for just a moment. Then it was replaced with another frown, as if she caught herself.

"Of course it sounds good. This all sounds really great and like a wonderful dream. But first of all, I run a ranch that has live animals on it, so I can't just up and run off to the beach whenever I want. I have responsibilities. Besides that, everything you're suggesting sounds like a full-time job."

"It is. That's why I think you need a full-time camp host that lives on-site, taking care of the ranch and the camps while you're gone. And I've got just the people in mind. Josh and Brittany."

Her eyes widened. "The newlyweds?"

"Not just newlyweds. Josh is a recent college graduate with a degree in Park Administration, and evidently Brittany has experience in event planning."

"That girl is afraid of horses."

He chuckled. "True. But apparently she's good at organizing and scheduling. And Josh says she's really good with social media, which would help with the marketing side of our business venture."

"Our business venture?" She shook her head. "You seem to have this all figured out, don't you?"

He picked up her hand and laid a gentle kiss on the back of it. "I'm trying. Because that's what I do. I'm a details guy. I thrive on finding logical solutions, which makes all of the business stuff so easy to talk about it. It's the other part, the relationship stuff, that's harder for me. Because, Skye, none of that is logical. And none of it fits into any part of my compartmentalized brain. But it doesn't have to. Because it all fits perfectly in my heart."

She blinked, and tears sprang to her eyes.

Shit. He wasn't trying to make her cry.

"I know, that sounds gushy as hell. But dammit, whenever I'm around you, my brain goes to mush. All I can think about is you. And I start picking flowers and taking couple-selfies and doing all the things I generally mock other silly couples for doing."

She laughed. A small laugh, barely a chuckle, but it was a start.

He reached up and cupped her cheek in the palm of his hand. "I don't know how to do all of this romantic stuff. Nor do I know if all of these ideas will work. I don't know what it will be like to fly back and forth to see each other, and I seriously have no idea how to help raise a kid, but I do know one thing—one crazy wonderful realization. I know that I'm in love with you. The rest is just details. And I'm good at handling those."

She wasn't saying anything, but she wasn't pulling away, either, and her body had relaxed, so he plunged ahead.

He slid his hand around the back of her neck and pulled her face to him. Leaning his forehead against hers, his voice broke. "I know you told me last night to go away and leave you alone. But the thought of walking out of your life terrifies me. A week ago, I couldn't possibly imagine spending my life with a cowgirl in Colorado, and now I can't imagine spending my life without her. Without you."

He swallowed. "Please say something."

"I don't know what to say," she whispered. "You have rendered me completely speechless."

He grinned. "Then how about you don't say anything and just kiss me?"

She slid her arms around his neck and pressed her lips to his. Words didn't matter when she kissed him like this.

Her fingers entwined in his hair as he pulled her tightly against him. If he'd had any question left about his feelings for her, they disappeared in the instant she wrapped her arms around him and her lips touched his.

Because in that moment, he knew he was home.

• • •

Skye didn't know how to respond, didn't know what to say. This had never happened to her before. But she had to say something.

Breaking the kiss, she pulled back and swiped at the tears that had fallen down her cheeks. His simple but beautiful words touched her soul and knit together the pieces of a heart that she had previously thought had been broken beyond repair.

Holding his face in her hands, his adorable, handsome face, she swallowed back the emotion blocking her throat.

Her heart pounded against her chest, and she took a deep shuddering breath. "Thank you. Thank you for liking my son and for working so hard to come up with all of these wonderful ideas. Thank you for what you did in my office—the mug, and the flowers, and the pictures. Oh my God, the pictures almost did me in. I loved them so much. Thank you for not giving up on me when I pushed you away and for holding on to me when I tried to leave.

"I love that you can always make me laugh. And I love that even when I pushed you away, you still came through for me and for my son. I didn't think I was capable of trusting another man with my heart. Heck, I wasn't sure if my heart still even worked, but I guess it does, because I can feel it pounding against my chest. It may be bruised, and battered, and a little out of shape, but it is yours, Adam Clark. Because I am crazy in love with you, and I'm giving it to you, completely, no-holds-barred. Because I know now that you will take care of it, take care of me, and take care of Cody."

She thought it would be harder when she decided to trust someone again, but it seemed to be the easiest thing she'd done all day. And suddenly the heavy burden that she'd carried all of these years—the chains that had kept her heart hidden away—disappeared. And she felt like she could finally breathe.

"You can trust me, Skye. I won't let you down."

"I know. I believe you. I love all your ideas, and I think we should go for it. Because I can't imagine my life without you in it, either. I want you to stay here with us, but when you go back to California, I know you'll come back."

"I will. I will always come home to you."

"I know. I love you, Adam. And I trust you."

And she really did.

Epilogue

One Year Later

Skye leaned against the fence, watching as the bus full of new campers pulled up to the ranch. This was the second group that had participated in their *Gaming and Grit* program. The first week had been a tremendous success.

The website and Facebook page that Brittany had set up was full of great reviews and filled with photos of campers participating in parts of a live-action video game.

Brittany had turned out to be surprisingly adept at social media and was quite skilled at the computer, instigating a new online registration system and a slew of new programming ideas.

She and Josh now lived in the apartment in the lodge, and they'd been a huge help running the ranch while Skye and Cody spent time in California.

Adam had hired a local construction company to build a beautiful custom log home on the west side of the property, and they'd moved in earlier that spring. They had privacy but were still within a five-minute walk of the ranch. And with all of the technology he'd added, Adam could do a lot of work remotely, so he tried to spend as much time at the new house as he could.

They had worked tirelessly that year, putting the new plans for the ranch into play, but they'd also made time for fun.

She and Cody had flown to California several times, and Adam had taken them to Disneyland and to the Caribbean earlier in the year. They'd split holidays between the two houses but had spent Christmas in Colorado, where, with the snow-topped Rockies in the background, Adam had proposed.

Skye smiled down at the diamond ring adorning her left hand. The wedding was scheduled for late August, just when the aspens were starting to change.

They planned to get married in Colorado, at the ranch, where they'd first met and fallen in love.

It seemed like so long ago. She never could have imagined that a ridiculously smart computer engineer from California who wore glasses and faded Converse sneakers would fit so easily into a dude ranch in Colorado and into their lives. But he did, and it was amazing.

She'd never laughed so much in her life as she had in the last year. Adam and Cody were always up to something. They were as close as any real father and son, and the papers had already been filed for Adam to legally adopt him.

They were a real family. A family of three that, after the positive test she'd taken that morning, was about to grow to four.

She hadn't told Adam yet. She was saving it as a surprise to share after tonight's hay ride. But she knew he'd be thrilled.

Because she knew Adam. Knew him. Loved him. Trusted him.

She pushed off the fence, a smile breaking across her face as she rubbed a hand lightly over her belly, and went to greet the new campers.

THE END…

…AND JUST THE BEGINNING

Acknowledgments

As always, my love and thanks goes out to my husband, Todd, for your steadfast love and support in my writing career and in our life together! We make the best team!

Huge thanks to my Entangled sisters, Beth Rhodes and Cindy Skaggs, who helped make this work possible through their constant support and lots and lots of writing sprints—whether I wanted to do them or not. Your accountability and support is invaluable!

Special thanks to Kristin Miller for your plotting help. Your friendship and encouragement mean the world to me.

Many thanks to my editor, Brenda Chin, for your awesome editing talents. And buckets of thanks to the whole Entangled Publishing team for all of your efforts and hard work in making this book happen.

Special acknowledgement goes out to the women that walk this writing journey with me every day. The ones that make me laugh, who encourage and support, who offer great advice and sometimes just listen. Thank you Michelle Major, Lana Williams, Anne Eliot, Ginger Scott, and Selena Laurence. XO

About the Author

USA TODAY Bestselling author Jennie Marts loves to make readers laugh as she weaves stories filled with love, friendship and intrigue. Reviewers call her books "laugh out loud" funny and full of great characters.

She is living her own happily ever after in the mountains of Colorado with her own Prince Charming. She's addicted to Diet Coke, adores Cheetos, and believes you can't have too many books, shoes, or friends.

Her books include the following series: the Hearts of Montana, the Page Turners, the Bannister Brothers Books, and the Cotton Creek Romances.

Jennie loves to hear from readers. Follow her on Facebook at Jennie Marts Books, or Twitter at @JennieMarts. Visit her at www.jenniemarts.com.

Discover the* Cotton Creek Romance *series…

ROMANCING THE RANGER

HOOKED ON LOVE

Also by Jennie Marts

TUCKED AWAY

HIDDEN AWAY

STOLEN AWAY

Find love in unexpected places with these satisfying Lovestruck reads...

The Hook Up

a *First Impressions* novel by Tawna Fenske

Content with her booming career as a purveyor of Madame Butterfly pleasure aids, Ellie Sanders doesn't need a man for anything—except maybe marketing tips. And, okay, a few fun nights with something that doesn't require batteries. Enter Tyler Hendrix. The Navy helped Ty put his tumultuous childhood behind him, but when sexy single mom Ellie walks through the First Impressions door looking for a way to take her business to the next level, their scorching sexual attraction threatens to crumble Tyler's walls for good...

A Taste of You

a *Bourbon Boys* novel by Teri Anne Stanley

Good thing Eve likes a challenge. That's exactly what she'll face trying to convince a flaky contractor's hunky son to tackle the distillery's visitor center so she can cross another item off her very organized to-do list. Commitment-phobe carpenter Nick Baker can't resist helping sexy Eve out of her jam. But, her addictive, forever-flavored kisses push him out of his caution zone, and if he's not careful his past will nail him to the wall.

Just One Week

a novel by Alice Gaines

Her brother's best friend is not only the hottest man Michelle Dennis has ever seen, he's the reason she left town eight years ago. Of *course* he's the one waiting at the airport. Worse, he made sure they're staying in the same house. Keeping his hands *off* is a test Alex Stafford is bound to fail, but falling in love isn't an option, and remembering that will save them both a lot of heartache...

Made in the USA
Lexington, KY
18 April 2018

CATCHING the COWGIRL

California video game designer Adam Clark knows that, in h
business, authenticity is the key. So, for their newest Wester
adventure game, he and his partners decide to try out
Cowboy Camp. Only Adam's friends never arrive, leaving him
bit—okay, *a lot*—preoccupied, trying to resist the gorgeous
cowgirl who owns the ranch.

Single mom Skye Hawkins is too busy trying to keep her famil
dude ranch out of the red to even think about romance. Bu
she's having trouble avoiding Adam. He's smart, he's sweet, h
funny…and he's hot! Maybe it's the mountain air, but she fin
herself letting down her guard. And the fireworks are definite
worth it.

The only problem—they live in totally different worlds. Still,
Adam is nothing if not resourceful. Sure, he wants to catch t
cowgirl. But more importantly,
he needs to find a way to keep her.